LEXI GREENE

Bachelor on Trial

Second edition

ISBN: 978-0-6451127-1-9

This book was professionally typeset on Reedsy.
Find out more at reedsy.com

# Contents

# Foreword

When Tony Radcliff joins Forbes lawyers, career-driven Scarlet O'Connor finds she has competition for the coveted partnership position.

And Tony has a couple of aces up his sleeve. Like his surf-sculpted body, which plays havoc with Scarlet's 'all work and no play' plans for partnership. And his brother, who holds the key to a secret from her past.

When Scarlet and Tony start steaming up the office windows, there's no doubt they're playing with fire. But there can only be one winner, so who gets burned?

# Acknowledgement

A huge thank you to my editor Jena O'Connor, my proofreader Janice Owen, and my cover designer Charmaine Ross! And to the gorgeous Joanne Dannon, Beverley Eikli and Nina Campbell for their endless support. And thank you to my lovely hubby, Steve, who inspired me to write this story, and to my precious lovelies, Mia and Dan.

# Chapter One

Scarlet focused on her breath and not the deep mahogany of the lift doors in front of her. Or the metal on metal clanging of its inner workings. Or the hands of her watch as they circled closer to seven. She breathed in until her chest felt full and her belly expanded. Breathed out—slow and steady. Her phone pinged and she glanced at the screen. *You've got this.* The reminder went off at seven every morning and every morning she stood frozen; her body paralysed in a percussion of protest. *You can do this.*

The lift doors parted, and the mirror-clad, marble-floored cavity waited for her to enter. Simple. One step, then another. Press level ten. She could do this. She'd done it before. She just had to acknowledge the reaction, breathe through it and step into the small, tight, enclosed chamber.

*Or take the stairs.* Her eyes veered to the side. The stairs were good for her thighs. Her buttocks, too. They were a cardio-vascular win-win.

Her high heels met the marble floor of the foyer with a confident *Hi, I'm Scarlet O'Connor, senior associate at Forbes Lawyers*. She reached for the fire escape door handle, but her grip slipped, and she had to shove it with her shoulder.

The stairs had become an important part of her morning

morphosis. *Toughen up, Scarlet. You've got this, Scarlet. You can do this, Scarlet.*

She eyed the spiralling, concrete stairway. One step at a time. The door banged behind her and her heart did that thing where it wanted to vacate the premises. Her throat tightened and her eyes took a moment to adjust to the sharp slap of the lighting and the raw tang of the concrete. She took a sip of the coffee she'd bought from Hudsons Coffee on Little Collins St. and breathed in the sweet undertones of vanilla and hazelnut... *the journey of a thousand miles begins with a single step.* One step at a time. There were no shortcuts to the top. With every step of the seventeen-times-ten stairs and landings, her skin hardened, crystallised and set until she morphed into the confident, professional, sophisticated—albeit a smidgen sweaty—woman who strode down the carpeted hallway to her not-yet-corner office. She wrenched the door open; her heart heaving a Thank God and lowered her only cup of coffee for the next twelve hours onto her desk.

There were files stacked high on every flat surface and floor to ceiling windows. The city of Melbourne stretched before her feet. She liked looking down on the already busy streets, and the early morning sunshine promised another warm summery day. She booted up her computer. Her crammed schedule flashed before her and she kicked off her heels.

A new senior associate had been hired to help with the files teetering on her desk, and they had a site visit in Myrniong first thing. She eyed the precarious stack, unwilling to give any of them away. The last thing she needed was more competition for the partnership opportunity due to be decided by the end of the financial year in less than four months. She took off her jacket and the black lettering on the inside of her wrist caught her attention—PS. The tattoo had come to represent her goal… PartnerShip… a goal as indelibly inscribed into her brain tissue as it was on her skin.

Partnership had come to represent more than professional success. It was about being on the top of the stack instead of the bottom. It was about feeling strong on the inside and erasing for always the fear of being powerless…

"Good morning." A male voice interrupted her thoughts. Low and rumbling like thunder before a storm front. "I'm Tony. Tony Radcliff. Dan told me you'd be in by seven fifteen. It's great to meet you."

Scarlet's coffee splashed out of the cup and onto the skirt of her suit. Hell. She mopped it up with tissues and glared at the cheerful man who had appeared in her doorway. No one, no one messed with her first hour in the office. She liked the quiet. She liked the company of her coffee, her calendar, and her to-do list. She didn't do cheerful. She didn't do camaraderie. Wait up. Did he say, Radcliff? She eyed the arresting blue eyes and the tan that said *he* didn't waste his weekends working. A barely-there recognition feathered her skin with a thousand tiny bug feet and slid down her spine.

"This is my power hour. I share it with no one. Come back after eight thirty if you want polite." She lowered her gaze to the file now open on her desk, but the words ran together, and those tiny bug feet became a tap-dancing torrent that roared in her ears.

"Dan suggested we collaborate on the Cartwright matter. If you could point to the file, I'll get familiar with it." There was no hint of offence in his tone. Instead, he sounded confident. Cocky. Unabashed.

Scarlet dragged her attention from her work. Her gaze

3

collided with his—steel coated in friendly. He'd been head-hunted by the firm, which meant he was good. He looked the part, too. Sharp grey suit. Snappy red tie. Smug expression. "Who let you in?"

"Bob organised my security pass when I came in on Friday. Nice bloke."

Easy fodder for the likes of a Radcliff. Well, she wasn't a fool and she knew his type. Good looking, athletic and fabulous, at least in his own eyes, with an ego that shouted I'm-the-best.

"I came in early to set up my office. I'm across the hall." Two dimples creased his clean-shaven face and the power of them hit her square in the chest.

In an office with no view. The thought smoothed the edges from her tone. "Then I'm sure Dan explained the lay of the land."

"We're on the same team, Scarlet." The smile lines around his eyes softened and she felt the magnetic pull of his personality. But her armour had been honed over one hundred and seventy stairs and she was as impervious as stone.

"Great." She closed the file in front of her and handed it over. "The site visit starts at ten thirty. See you downstairs at nine. It's a bit of a drive."

Dismissed, Tony thought. He reached for the file and noticed a tiny tattoo on the inside of her wrist. Interesting. Her glossy blonde hair was pulled back into a sleek ponytail giving her a youthful look, but her violet gaze said mature-woman and it clawed him with no apology. Intriguing. Her silk shirt, a soft grey in colour, and the pink sheen of her lips said feminine, but the steely rod in her back said strong, smart and I surrender to no one. Impressive. He took the file and strode away. He had less than two hours to get familiar with the matter, but he couldn't resist a glance back at the now closed glass door to her office. Already, her attention was back on her computer screen. There weren't too many women who met him and didn't show a flicker of interest in the depths of their eyes… and there weren't too many women who brought a flicker of interest to his own.

Scarlet O'Connor was competitor number one. He wasn't here to make friends. He was here to make partner. He understood her animosity. He knew her reputation. But if she wanted the partnership position, and he knew she did, then she'd have to fight him for it. His father had made partner by thirty years of age and it was a yardstick he'd held high for both of his sons. Not easy following in the footsteps of a High Court Judge nor being the youngest of his two boys by a long shot of twenty years. Not easy for Tony to watch his formidable father succumb to early-onset dementia. The one thing that brought a light to his father's eyes was the hope that Tony would succeed where his brother had failed. *No pressure, Ant.* Ant—Geoffrey called him that to make him feel small and all the hairs on his body bristled at the thought. He didn't give a fig about his brother, but his father? Even a year ago, he couldn't have cared less, but now? Now, time was running out and it was unclear how much longer his father would even recognise him, let alone appreciate the achievement… but, it had become important.

"I'll meet you in the foyer." Scarlet appeared in his doorway. Beyond a soft lip gloss, she didn't wear makeup, which was unusual in a law office. Women usually glammed up like bait on a hook. Her features were neat and symmetrical, her face heart-shaped, but he wouldn't call her beautiful, mostly because of the cold disdain of her expression, yet still, his lungs grappled for oxygen. Her black skirt hugged her hips and she wore a matching suit jacket. Her legs were long, and her heels were high. Her complexion was that of a soft peach, but she was dynamite and just as dangerous to mess with. He dragged his gaze from the violet trap of her eyes and checked the time. Eight fifty. How long did it take to go down in the lift?

"At nine, right?"

"Yes. You're one of Judge Radcliff's boys?"

"Yes." So, she'd done her homework. And he'd done his. He was still reeling from the law magazine articles he'd discovered on the internet. How old had she been at the time? Nineteen? He'd been on an overseas gap year, but he'd heard of the affair that broke his brother's marriage. Interesting to meet the scarlet woman responsible.

"Must be tough being the youngest."

"Makes you tough being the youngest. What about you? Any siblings?"

"None." She considered him, her gaze steady. "You've no doubt done some research of your own." The violet grey of her eyes turned gun-metal cold. "The past doesn't define me. If you've got a problem with it, talk to me."

"But not before eight thirty."

"We might get along, Radcliff. I'll see you downstairs in eight minutes."

When she turned to leave, he noted her lovely calves and tight arse. She worked out? When? From what he'd heard, she spent every waking moment in the office. He picked up his notes, then sat down again. He'd be there. But not a damn minute before nine o'clock. As ordered.

# Chapter Two

**W**here was he? Punctuality had been drummed into Scarlet from an early age. *It's a sign of respect, Carly. Everyone's time is important.*

Scarlet paced; her nerves stretched like elastic pulled to its limit. Tony Radcliff had brought back the past in vivid colour, and her insides quivered, her heart hammered, her head pounded. She retraced her steps and saw Bob at the security counter. He was older than her by a good forty years, his hair silver, his uniform a navy blue.

"How are you, Bob? How's the arthritis?"

"Alright thanks, Scarlet. Where are you off to?"

"A site visit. A winery near Myrniong. There was a workplace accident there about a year ago."

"Nice day for a drive in the country."

He was right. She just had to keep the jagged glass shards of the fractured skylight and the broken man on the flagstone floor of the winery restaurant out of her mind, at least until she got there. "Yes, it's a tough job." She glanced at her watch.

The lift doors opened, and Tony appeared. Maybe it was the metallic sigh of its workings or the closed-in space behind him, or maybe it was his saccharine smile—the way his cheeks dimpled, the whiteness of his teeth—but her skin contracted and the air around her seemed to tighten like a fist around her windpipe.

"Nice to see you again, Bob. How's your day going?" Tony's voice was like warm caramel over sticky date pudding and the older man's face brightened.

"So far, so good. Thanks for asking."

Scarlet's spine lengthened an inch and her hand tightened around her keys. "We need to go. See you, Bob. Have a good day."

She stormed towards the stairs to the basement. Her car was one level down. No point taking the lift. No point checking to see if he-who-thought-he-was-fabulous had followed. No point pondering the fact that he annoyed her. His charming, nice-guy smile was like a decadent chocolate dessert, too sweet after a couple of mouthfuls. His cheerful blue eyes were like sunshine after a big night out. Too bright. Too shiny. Too summer sky clear. The thought of an hour in close confines with Tony Radcliff brought hives to her skin. She pushed through the door and held it open for him. Along with punctuality, manners had been drummed into her. "One floor down. Turn to the left."

"In my world, men hold doors open for women."

He was the chivalrous type? "In my world, men aren't that necessary." She tapped her foot, her insides tangled... time was ticking.

He went to move past her, stopped—too close. Too damn close, sucking the oxygen from the air. "I know about your altercation with Geoffrey, but it was a long time ago and I promise you, I'm not like my brother." His blue gaze steadied on hers, easy and breezy, with just a hint of cloud. "Are you planning on holding that against me?"

"It was. I am. Are you planning to move anytime soon?"

8

"Fine." He stepped through the open space and took the stairs with athletic grace. Her nose scrunched against the warm waft of musky male scent. No sweet or spicy aftershave to dilute the power of him. She eyed his tight arse. His thick mop of brown hair, streaked with blond where the sun had bleached it. He was tall, lean and marginally attractive. Her fingers loosened on the door and it slammed shut. The sound echoed like a gunshot and blasted the madness from her thoughts.

"My turn." He stood on the landing below, his arm outstretched, the door open. His blue gaze challenged and for a furious moment, she found herself mesmerised. The moment seemed to stretch and elongate, and stopped her heart for long enough to hear the thud of his.

"Thanks." She pushed past him and strode towards her black Mercedes convertible. She loved it with a passion, the kind most women lavished on clothes or a cute canine. She'd saved until she could pay cash—she wasn't a credit kind of girl—and every time she pressed the lock release and the sound echoed in the cavernous space, her soul settled, and her heart sighed. Manners dictated she wait for Tony to get in and buckle his seatbelt before she turned the key, but manners were over-rated when it came to arrogant men. She breathed in the scent of the soft, creamy leather seats and revved the engine. Just a smidge.

Tony was one significant blemish on her escape plan. She adjusted the sound system to slightly higher than too-loud-for-conversation and hoped he'd get the message, but it seemed he was impervious to subtlety.

"Where did you get your law degree?"

"Melbourne University." Her attention was diverted by the aeronautical precision required to navigate the car park. Vehicles were slotted into the cramped space like jigsaw pieces.

"I went to Monash."

"Ah." Scarlet opened the window and waved her pass at the control panel. The boom-gate rose, and she ventured out into the snarl of traffic on Flinders Lane. Roadworks further along had caused a backlog of traffic. She was aware of Tony beside her and it wasn't the good kind of awareness. It was the kind that left her strung out like a juror delivering a guilty verdict. Her lungs snatched at the tight air. She had to force her breathing to slow, her grip on the smooth leather steering wheel to loosen. She allowed the soothing wash of her favourite classical music—violins, piano, double bass—to ease the wound-up crazy in her body.

"Where did you work before Forbes?" He turned to her, his elbow on the open window ledge, aviator sunglasses on his nose, looking as relaxed and casual as if he had a right to be there.

It seemed he wanted to talk. She found small talk effortful and the thought of having to chat with Tony for the next hour chafed like bare legs on a hot leather seat. "I did articles at Forbes and never left."

"Ah, that explains the office with a window."

"I bring in more income than three associates put together."

"Good to know." He grinned and the sun flashed on his teeth.

Clever. Conniving. Wolf—in one hundred percent fine wool—just like his older brother. She'd walked right into it. He was a snake in the grass. A crocodile in a swamp, its eyes breaking the water. He could *not* be trusted. She clamped her teeth and edged into the lane of traffic for the Westgate Bridge. She settled her own sunglasses onto her nose and welcomed the relief from the glare.

"How often do you go out to views?"

"Occasionally. It helps to see the space where the worker was injured. This guy fell through the skylight despite the safety equipment provided for the roof work he was doing."

"Why insurance litigation?"

"I could ask you the same." If she was interested, which she wasn't. She raised the volume, desperate for the peace that usually flooded her when she listened to Mozart. The traffic was heavy, and the light in front of her changed from amber to red. Damn. She hated traffic. She hated waiting. She hated that Tony sat beside her, relaxed and cool in his seat. No rigidity in his muscles. No bulging tendons in his neck. No angry snapping anywhere in his body.

"Are you always like this in traffic?"

"Yes." This had nothing to do with the man beside her—or his older brother—and everything to do with him wanting what was hers. Breathe. She moved through her body relaxing each part until she could feign ease. She focused on the vast blue stretch of the sky and pictured herself somewhere sunny, the relaxing sound of water spilling over rocks, no one for miles.

"Light's green when you're ready."

His tone was provocative, but she refused to bite. "Thanks." A horn tooted from somewhere behind them. She pressed her foot to the clutch and eased into first. She liked a manual. She liked the rev of the engine. The feel of the gearstick in her hand. She changed into second... third... and back into second as they approached the Westgate Bridge in a snarl of trucks and vans and other vehicles. The view was spectacular, and if she could just focus on the world around her and not on the pair of hard, muscular thighs not a hand's breadth away, she'd find it easier to breathe. The music wasn't helping. The mindfulness strategies weren't helping. The gutsy thrust of acceleration

11

wasn't helping.

"You seem kind of wound up."

No kidding. "I'm not very patient with traffic and I'm frustrated that I have competition for a position that's rightfully mine. And given who you are, there's little chance of a fair fight."

"Competition stretches us and makes us stronger." His gaze turned towards the horizon and the blue haze of the sea.

Her grip tightened until her knuckles turned white. She checked her speed and throttled down... there were speed cameras on the bridge. "Is that what your father taught you?"

"Pretty much."

"Did he pit you and your brother against each other? A bit of healthy sibling rivalry?"

"You get further in life when you're challenged."

Scarlet risked a disbelieving glance. "Is that what he told you?" Tony looked straight ahead, but there was a tick in his jaw, like his teeth ground together. That was a lot of pressure. "How far are you aiming to get?"

"Partner. Executive partner. Maybe start my own firm."

The jittery sensation inside her moved from snappy to grabby. "Timeframe?"

"Partner by thirty. The rest will fall into place."

They passed Williamstown on the left and reached the one hundred kilometre an hour zone. She couldn't wait to get out on the open road. "How long until you're thirty?"

"Less than twelve months."

Scarlet was good at maths, but she didn't need to be... their career trajectories were on a collision course. He didn't know what he was up against. "Why Forbes?"

"It's a small, but highly reputable firm."

"Why insurance litigation?"

"My brother is a commercial lawyer."

Scarlet glanced into her side mirror, moved into the left lane. "You don't see yourself on the same path as your brother?"

"No." He turned to look at her. "I'm nothing like my brother."

"I'm glad to hear it, but there's only one partnership opportunity likely to come up in the next twelve months." She was stuck behind a lumbering truck and her speed slowed, frustration curling her toes.

"May the best man—or woman—win."

Smug. Slimy. Snake.

She went to pass the truck, but it pulled out in front of her and she had to touch the brakes. His driving was atrocious. His manners were worse. She flipped the disk to Vivaldi and took a deep, calming breath. And sat tight until they were on the slip road, where she slowed for long enough to retract the roof before pressing her foot to the accelerator. The rush of air helped to relieve the organ-crushing squeeze in her midriff, and then they were onto the M80, and she shifted into fifth gear.

"What do you like to do on the weekends?"

Scarlet glanced at Tony. With his aviators on and the wind blowing his hair back from his face, he looked... attractive, or at least he would have if she hadn't been so set on finding him unattractive. "Work. You?"

Curses. She hadn't meant to sound interested. She wasn't interested. She turned her attention back to the road and breathed deeply of the fresh, almost country air, the tension in her body blasted away. The temperature was warm, not too hot, and it was impossible not to relax and enjoy the responsive surge of the V8 motor.

"I like to surf."

Well, that explained the tan and the relaxed cheeriness that rubbed against her like sandpaper. He had a lackadaisical, beach-bum attitude to life that didn't quite fit with the polished, corporate sheen of his suit. Or what she knew of his family.

"Why would a layback surfer dude want to become a hotshot lawyer?" She made no attempt to soften the mocking tone.

"The two aren't mutually exclusive and you know enough about my family to appreciate the pressure. Besides, you manage to pull off the conservative, uptight workaholic in the office when you're clearly a weekend lead-foot in a black convertible." He grinned and she hoped he got a bug in his pristine white teeth.

"We all have our vices."

"I wouldn't have taken you for a rev-head."

Her gaze snapped to his side of the vehicle.

"I'm not judging." He held his hands up, his grin widening.

There was no way she was going to let him mess with her joy. She tried to erase him from her peripheral vision and pretend she was alone. Except he insisted on speaking.

"I spend my weekends in Torquay. You know what they say about all work and no play. Maybe that explains how you found yourself in that awkward position in the first place... no pun intended."

Not listening.

"Don't tell me you're one of those types who doesn't like the feel of sand on your feet." He turned towards her and lifted his sunglasses.

Not listening.

"Or one of those girls who can't bear to get their hair wet."

His gaze burned into the side of her face like a brand.

Not listening.

14

"Or someone who's wedded to their work because they have no life."

Pow. He finished with a punch and her stomach clenched. "It's nice of you to worry about me, but there's no need. We're work colleagues. The only thing you need to worry about is how well I do my job, and that's very well." She flicked the indicator and accelerated past a slower vehicle, the motor eager and responsive. "Have you had any run-ins with sharks while you're out there in the elements?"

"None of the fish variety." He settled his glasses on his nose and his elbow on the window frame.

"Ha. Ha." Her thoughts followed the path he'd guided her down. Was she wedded to her work because she didn't have a life? Or did she not have a life because she was wedded to her work? Or was he trying to mess with her focus? He wanted that partnership position. He wanted it enough to manipulate and undermine her while wearing a goofy smile on his face. Speaking of sharks.

"Perhaps we should talk about the elephant in the back seat and get it out in the open."

"There's no elephant, Tony. Mistakes are learning opportunities. I've learned that men don't always tell the truth about their marital status. I've learned that some men have an ego so big they don't understand the meaning of the word no, and I've learned that some men think they're above the law. Do you go home to a wife at night?"

"So glad you brought that up. I'm single in capital letters—in case, you're interested—but I plan to stay that way until I make partner. I can't afford the distraction of a serious relationship. You?"

"I don't do distraction. My goal is partnership. And I want it

15

within the year. And no, I'm not *interested*."

His grin widened. "What about family? Do you want children someday?"

Damn him. She wished he'd back off with his questions. She wished she could call him an Uber and tell him to meet her there. Better still, she'd like to rewind time and schedule the view for yesterday, so she'd have her V8 sanctuary to herself instead of being forced to share it with a Great White Career-killer in Hugo Boss.

She shrugged and left the question unanswered, her gaze seeking the horizon.

"I can't wait to have kids. I want them to run free on the beach and have fun in the surf. I want weekend barbies with friends, and a glass of wine with someone special on the deck of our beach house after the kids are tucked into bed, exhausted, with smiles on their faces."

"Is that what your childhood was like?" She turned and saw tension in the set of his jaw.

"Not so much. My brother's twenty years older than me and my father worked a lot. I used to go down to Lorne with a friend of mine. His parents had a house that looked over the ocean and they taught me to surf. I loved those family trips and they treated me like a son."

Her heart softened for the boy he used to be, and she had to remind herself of the man he was now. "I'm an only child." No way would she share the loneliness of her childhood. They began the descent into the valley that was Bacchus Marsh. The earth was rich and fertile and apple trees spread before them. Market gardens, turf farms. She toyed with the idea of a detour through the town on the way back for fresh fruit and gourmet chocolate from the roadside, farm-direct stores.

"Did you have extended family?"

"An older cousin, but he was like the big brother from hell." She fought the memory of her eight-year-old self and *that* game of hide-and-seek. She'd hidden from her cousin in a wardrobe in their spare room and he'd turned the key in the lock leaving her trapped, paralysed and afraid in the dark, cramped, airless space. She'd counted to a thousand, her eyes squeezed shut, and she hadn't called for help because she didn't want him to know how scared she was, but then she'd peed her pants in panic.

Sweat beaded on her brow and she welcomed the cool rush of the wind. She gulped oxygen into her lungs and focused on the wide, open space around her, forcing back the hot, choking memory. "I hated visiting them. I preferred to be alone. I liked to read. Besides, I had good friends and mum often invited one of them to go on holiday with us."

"Are you okay?" His tone sounded sincere.

"Yes, fine. Thanks. You?" She turned towards him.

"Terrific."

He looked terrific and for the shortest flash of a moment, she admired him. He was smart. Well-connected. Gorgeous—well, passably attractive. And she felt a connection. *Sever it. Now.* This was about weakening her. He didn't care. He was figuring out what he was up against. Steel. She visualised it. Cold and impervious.

"You don't like to let people in, do you?"

"I've learned that most people are self-serving, particularly men." They left the fertile ground of the valley behind and wound their way into the dry, windswept hills. A house perched on a barren knoll, the driveway like a scar across the landscape.

"That's very cynical."

"Perhaps."

He sat taller in his seat and shifted his attention to her face. "Do you bat for the other team now? After your run in with Geoffrey?"

"Pardon?"

"Are you a girl's girl now?"

"No!" She almost choked. "And even if I was, it's none of your damn business." He was like a blood-sucking leech. "If there's something work related you need to know, ask. If not? Don't. Speak."

"You're not an easy person to like." He settled back into slouch-mode and tapped his leg in time with the music.

"I don't care whether you like me or not. I don't need your friendship. I need you like a bullet in the side of my head." In fact, she'd prefer the bullet over another moment in his company.

Silence. Blessed silence. The paddocks flashed past and the trees grew big and wide and spread their limbs to the sky. Space. Lots of it. And silence. But try as she might, she couldn't ignore him. It was like an invisible string stretched between them and every time he breathed or shifted in his seat, it pulled tight and she reacted, deep inside.

"You weren't the first young receptionist to be dazzled by Geoffrey's charms, and he no doubt plied you with plenty of alcohol. You *were* the first to sue him, expose him in the media and destroy his marriage."

She said nothing, but her heart contracted. She'd been dewy fresh and naïve when she'd started work at a top-tier law firm during her gap year. Her hands clenched on the steering wheel. She'd bought her first V8 convertible with the pay-out. Unfair dismissal. She'd honed her legal teeth on that one and she'd been like a dog with a bone. Where other students had struggled to learn the dry tenements of law, she'd devoured them, armouring herself with legal know-how to fight the battle against him.

"I'm guessing men give you a wide berth at the office Christmas party." His tone was as dry as the grassy fields that spread before them. She had to admire his tenacity. Most people knew of the assault. It had been splashed through the papers after she broke the gag order when he reneged on his side of the negotiations. Geoffrey Radcliff had been twice her age and powerful enough in the industry to intimidate her. But not many people had the balls to bring it up.

"He made it out to be consensual—maybe it was at first—but that requires a level of sobriety." She'd flirted back. She'd enjoyed the attention. But when he'd pushed her into the lift and stopped it between floors, her brain had fried. She couldn't get out. She couldn't scream. Who would have heard her? He'd kissed her and forced his tongue into her mouth. He'd touched her intimately, his hands venturing under her clothing, and he'd pressed her into the wall of the lift, his erection rubbing against her until—she'd found the strength to push him back. She shuddered. She'd been *Pissed* and *Stupid* at *nineteen*, and she'd lost her job because of it. She'd been *Powerless* and *Slandered*.

"The legal process has a way of shaming the victim."

"Yes…" But the victim became *Powerful* like the V8 motor that purred beneath her hands. And the victim became *Strong* and found her voice. No way would she shrink in the dark or suffer in silence again. "But the victim was victorious in the end."

"Is that why you work so hard? Do you still have something to prove?"

"Why do you care, Radcliff? Can't you sit back and enjoy the scenery?"

"Oh, I am, believe me."

19

She turned and found his sizzling blue gaze on *her*. Her skin prickled like every nerve had been plucked and played and a part of her body that had been safely anaesthetised for the past ten years, stirred and stretched. "I couldn't be less interested." The words should have been powerful and decisive with no room for misinterpretation, but he chuckled, and she found she liked it.

"I see you, Scarlet." His tone was a soft strum that resonated through her, and her skin puckered and pulled.

"I see you too, Radcliff. And if you think I'll fall for your scheming, you're wrong." She tightened her grip on the steering wheel.

"You think I'm strategizing and plotting?" He quirked an eyebrow above his aviator frames.

"Some men use seduction like a weapon."

"Some women are too cynical for their own good. There's a good chance you'll end up isolated and alone, with files for company."

"I have a V8 powered friend who asks for nothing." Stop. Flirting.

"Are we talking sex-toys here?"

"I don't know, Radcliff. You're the player. You tell me."

"Don't let my brother destroy your life. You didn't ruin his. He did that all by himself." The playful edge was gone from his tone, and if she hadn't had her attention on the road, she would have seen the serious light in his eyes. But she felt the shift in his muscle tension and when he reached out to touch her hand on the gear stick, she snatched it back, paralysis in her throat, the engine roaring in protest.

"I'm sorry, Scarlet. I get it. You don't like to be touched."

"I don't like to be taken advantage of. I don't like to be used.

I don't like to be played." And if Tony shared any of his older brother's genes, there was a good chance of all three.

"Then let's be honest with each other. As scathing as you like."

"I've been burned. I don't trust easily. It's that simple." Her heart pounded in her chest.

"Trust is earned. I don't expect you to trust me. You went through a terrible ordeal when you were younger at the hands of my arrogant shit of a brother." He shook his head. "When did you last have fun?"

"I'm too busy for fun." Tears welled up and blurred her vision, and she choked them back. She refused—refused—to show weakness in front of Tony Radcliff.

"Come down to Torquay with me. We could sit on the beach, feed chips to the seagulls, and stroll through the shallows. Better still, I could teach you to surf."

"Thanks for your concern and your offer, but no thanks." The sign for the Myrniong turn-off appeared and she sighed with relief. "Let's hope the engineer's on time."

"What's the claim worth, do you think?"

"Seven figures. The plaintiff's a quadriplegic and the Worksafe report is scathing." She strived to focus on the job ahead.

"You really don't like the beach?"

"I'm more of a shopping mall kind of girl." His words about honesty echoed in her head and she fought the recalcitrant need to be oppositional. "Fine. I like the beach. I used to fish with my dad. We had an old motorboat and I loved to drive it."

"Where did you go for your holidays?"

"Eden in New South Wales. I loved it there. We used to hike to the summit of Mt. Imlay, and we'd fish off the beach at Haycock Point. We'd build a huge fire on the sand and cook fish in foil. And we fished off the pier at the woodchip mill and took a four-wheel drive track out to Lennards Island to fish off the rocks. But there were eels there and I hated catching those." She shuddered. Even the thought of one twisting on the end of her line was disgusting.

"When did you last have a holiday?"

Tension snaked into her throat. "I don't remember."

"Don't the partners force you to take time off?"

"Yes, but I go into the office." She tightened her grip on the steering wheel and focused on avoiding the potholes in the gravel road that led to the winery.

"You don't think that's a bit obsessive?"

"I'm goal-oriented."

"Why is partnership so important to you?"

She sensed his scrutiny but kept her eyes on the road, which was more suited to a four-wheel drive SUV than a prestige luxury car. She slowed her speed to minimise the dust. Every pothole grabbed at the wheel and the stones flicked up making her flinch. "I made a promise to myself and my promises are golden."

"That's it?"

She didn't have to explain herself. She didn't have to explain how being at the lowest rung in a law firm had taught her something about power and the importance of it. Maybe it was the way his voice resonated inside her chest or maybe it was the way his tone pulled at that invisible string. Or maybe it was because he'd called his brother an arrogant shit, but she found herself telling him the truth. "I want to fast-track my career and have a family before I'm too old." Her history of painful periods and endometriosis meant she couldn't afford to waste time, but Scarlet was determined to make partner first. She wanted the respect and financial security that came with it, and she never wanted to feel powerless again. *What if you can't have children?* That was a possibility she refused to consider.

"What about a husband? Have you factored him in?"

"Not necessarily. I'm a realist." She shifted her attention to a particularly deep pothole in the road. "Ah, here it is."

The car park was empty, and she found a spot in the shade. The day was working its way towards hot and the scent of the eucalyptus trees was strong in the air. No sign of the engineer.

Scarlet cut the engine and sat motionless. She absorbed the sounds of the rosellas' chatter and the shriek of cockatoos as they flashed between the trees. She breathed the strong earthy scent that rose from the ground and savoured the feel of the breeze, soft against her face.

"What about you." She turned to observe him. "Why the urgency to become a partner by thirty?"

"Since we have a pact to speak the whole truth and nothing but the truth, and my word is golden..." His gaze held hers and she teetered on the blue, blue edge of it. Whispers of sadness lurked in the shadowy depths, defying the sunny flash of humour. "It's important to my father."

"And your father is important to you."

"Yes." He sounded surprised, like he hadn't expected her to get it. "There was a strong expectation that I study law, but I saw what it did to my brother. I took a year off and travelled through India, Spain, Turkey and some other countries. I didn't speak to my father for almost five years and I let him think I was overseas wasting my life, but in truth, I came back and studied. I surfed a lot and barely passed, but here I am."

"But you resolved the rift with your father?"

"Yes. I stayed in touch with my mum. She let me know he wasn't well. *She* wasn't well either, but I didn't know that until later." He took a deep breath, his gaze somewhere in the distance. "With time, I realised law was in my blood and it felt right."

"But you didn't want to follow the same path as your brother?"

"No." He glanced at her with a crooked smile. "I like to think I'm the black sheep of the family."

"That's not a bad thing, given what I know about Geoffrey. Shall we look around? The restaurant's closed on a Monday, but Richard, the owner, should be here." Scarlet opened her door and stepped out. She reached for the file and her notes from the boot and when Tony slammed the door behind him, she pressed her key and the roof slid back into place. She didn't want any hitchhikers of the bug variety.

"I've heard they do a great Cab Sav here." Tony's gaze was on the bluestone buildings not far ahead. There was a manicured green lawn and a rambling rose seemed to cover the entire portico. It was one of those old-fashioned varieties and the pink flowers had a sweet scent that travelled in undercurrents beneath the stronger scent of the native bushland.

"We're not here for the wine, Radcliff." Scarlet heard the crunch of wheels on gravel and turned back. "Oh, good. Here he is now."

A white Toyota Hilux pulled up beside her car. The door opened and a man in his mid to late sixties stepped out.

"Morning, Scarlet. And this must be Tony." He reached out to shake hands. "I'm Neil from Gray and Associates."

"Nice to meet you, Neil." Tony flashed a mega-watt smile.

Scarlet inwardly rolled her eyes. Tony was the kind of guy who won a bloke over with a grin and a warm handshake. She stepped forward and shook hands. "Hi, Neil. Thanks for coming."

"This was a nasty one."

"Sure was." They walked towards the buildings and two hours later, Scarlet realised Tony had gone AWOL. Where was he? She said her farewells to Neil and unlocked the car, storing her paperwork in the boot. She retracted the roof and turned towards the winery. Tony appeared around the corner of the restaurant carrying a box that jangled with bottles and his grin was wide.

"Perfect timing. Hope you don't mind if we put these in the back."

"You bought wine? How long ago did you ditch us?"

"I got talking to Richard and he was telling me about their latest award-winning Cab Sav and one thing led to another. It's an excellent drop. I invested in a dozen. Maybe we should crack one tonight. No doubt, we'll be working late."

"Emphasis on the word, working, Radcliff."

"Doesn't mean we can't enjoy ourselves."

He lowered the box into the back seat of the car and his grin created all kinds of havoc until the good kind of stirring in her body made way for the irritated kind. "Are you always this Pollyanna cheerful?" She plopped into her seat with a huff.

"Pretty much. No point being miserable."

"I like being miserable." She shifted her sunglasses further up her nose and revved the engine. No way would she tolerate friendly chit chat on the way back. She needed to think about the case and what they'd learned. She needed to keep her thoughts on work and resist the temptation of the man beside her. And she managed well until she saw the Bacchus Marsh exit and visions of farm-fresh fruit danced before her eyes. She glanced at the clock. They'd made good time. Why not?

# Chapter Three

The perfect purr of the engine changed to a rhythmic kathump and Scarlet felt the steering wheel pull to one side. They'd made it through the township of Bacchus Marsh and had started down the Avenue of Honour, where beautiful old trees bordered both sides of the road creating a shady canopy. Scarlet slowed down and the vehicle limped to the side of the road. A flat tyre? "I don't believe it. I've *never* had a flat tyre in this car." Travelling with Radcliff was like travelling with a small rain cloud over her head. She shouldn't have succumbed to the temptation of a detour.

"No problem. I can change a tyre."

His chest expanded with manly pride and Scarlet stifled a sigh. The last thing she needed was to be stranded with Tony Radcliff. "No need. I'll call roadside assist and get some tyre sealant."

His brows lifted in question.

"The car doesn't come with a spare tyre, Radcliff, so unless you've got some chewing gum handy to repair it, we're kind of stuck."

"No spare?"

"No spare."

"At least we have wine," he said with a grin and scrutinised the road ahead. "And I think I see one of those farm-direct roadside shops not far away. I'm thinking cheese, crackers, fruit… and chocolate. Dark chocolate coated orange slices. I wonder if they'll have those."

"Fine." Scarlet pulled out her mobile phone and hit the emergency number she had listed. "Maybe glasses too. I don't fancy slugging from a wine bottle."

"Your wish is my command."

"Hah!"

He grinned and strolled away, and she couldn't help but watch him go. The store looked to be one of the bigger establishments. Scarlet liked to support the local farmers. In truth, she came this way on her irregular visits to see her parents. They'd moved to Ballarat for a tree-change and she'd detoured a couple of times for fresh country produce. She loved the dappled shade from the avenue of trees and the orchards bordering the road. *It was a workday.* Her mind skittered to her jam-packed schedule. She didn't have time for this. She had a mediation at two and if this took longer than half an hour, she'd be late. At least she'd prepared her notes before they left.

Scarlet dialled the office and asked her legal assistant to postpone the mediation until later in the day. She glanced at her watch and scanned the rear-view mirror for flashing yellow lights. Nothing.

She pulled out her notebook and plotted her argument to support her client. Richard had been helpful, and she now had a good picture of the situation. The worker had climbed onto the roof in the rain to fix a leak and the tiles would have been slick, but they were broken and missing in places, and he may well have tripped. She tried not to think of the high price he'd paid.

Her phone pinged and she scrolled through her messages. She was on to her fourth return call when Tony approached, a brown shopping bag in his hand. He waved two plastic wine glasses in the air with a mischievous grin. Scarlet wound up her conversation and with her gaze glued to him, said her farewells. Her pulse leapt—skittish—and she couldn't quite temper the grin. "You're a magician."

"Oh, there's magic in this here bag," he said with a flourish. "Tell me you have a picnic rug in your boot, and I'll love you forever."

Scarlet toyed with the idea of lying. The thought of him loving her forever sat in her stomach like a too-starchy dish of pasta. Radcliff was a burr. A cheerful burr who'd burrowed into her peace and quiet with no apology. She flicked the automatic boot unlock and let him discover it for himself. She got out of the car and stretched out the kinks in her back.

He held it aloft and then bowed like a Shakespearean player. She had to laugh. It started low in her belly and bubbled up like expensive champagne. "What if the repair guy shows up?"

"We'll pour him a wine."

"You win." She pulled the brand new, never used rug from his hands and released the Velcro tape. She spread it out on the grassy verge, ditched her heels and sat. "I don't remember the last time I had a picnic."

"Ah, but this isn't just any old picnic. This is the platinum lounge of picnics." He poured her a red wine and held it out. "Try this."

"It's a workday, Radcliff."

"Try it and then tell me it's a workday."

She hated being told what to do, especially by a cocky man in an uber-expensive suit. She breathed in the earthy scents of black cherry and liquorice and took a small sip, savouring the full-bodied flavour. "You chose this?"

"Are you telling me you don't like it?"

His cheerfulness was contagious. She should be attached to her phone while she waited for help. Instead, passers-by could be forgiven for thinking this was a romantic tryst. She leaned back, her legs stretched in front of her, her feet bare, her toenails painted pink. Tony lay beside her on his side using a plastic knife to cut slices of cheese and pile them on crackers slathered with quince paste. He passed over a fully laden one for her to taste. "What do you think?"

She sank her teeth into the soft, creamy cheese, the saltiness contrasting with the sweetness of the quince paste. Both complimented the red wine to perfection. "It's good."

"It's better than good." His grin was armed and dangerous, and his dimples blew her resistance to smithereens. He was nothing like his older brother.

"Okay, it's amazing. Gorgeous. Outstanding. You're brilliant." Her heart sashayed against her ribs like a Burlesque dancer.

"That's better."

She eyed the spread before her. "There's chocolate."

"I know the way to a woman's heart."

It was a backhanded comment, yet the shadow of it erased the lightness that had radiated through her. He was a player. There was no doubt in her mind. He knew how to seduce. It ran in his genes. He seduced with every glib joke, every smirk, every probing question. The joy faded, the frivolity in her chest deflated and she took a sip of her wine to hide the disappointment. What did she care? It wasn't like she was stupid enough to fall for any of this anyway.

"What happened?"

"I don't know what you mean." She lifted her chin and took a deep breath of the fresh, grass-scented air. It was a beautiful day. A glorious day. And she refused to let him spoil it.

"You're stunning… when you smile. You know that?"

"Save it, Radcliff. Your moves are wasted on me. I'm not interested." Been there, done that with a Radcliff before, and she didn't need to make the same mistake to taste bitterness on her tongue.

"That's not what your eyes say."

His eyes said plenty too, but she wasn't listening. "My eyes don't know what's good for them."

"That's a pity. I kind of liked what they were saying."

"Whatever you think they were saying was coloured by whatever is going on in your own devious mind."

"There's nothing wrong with finding a colleague attractive."

"You're right and I find you *so* attractive," she mocked, her hand on her heart. "I can hardly hold myself back. It's lucky I'm already sitting down because when you look at me like that? My legs go weak and my lips crave one taste—one taste—of yours."

"Nice try, Scarlet."

She grinned and took a large bite of her cracker, but her gaze snagged on the jagged edge of his and awareness sparked between them. His gaze lowered and lingered on her lips like a caress—a silky, soft caress that raised the small hair follicles all over her body. Her own gaze dropped to his clean-shaven jaw. Strong and square. Her hand tingled with the need to touch and the imaginary warmth of his skin. Her gaze travelled a sensual path to the velvety texture of his lips. Her own lips yearned in response. What was wrong with her. Not. Going. To. Happen. Ever.

"Wait."

"What?"

He reached out and traced the line of her jaw, his touch lingering on her bottom lip. "You have a crumb."

If her resistance hadn't disintegrated like a puff of pink smoke, she would have swiped his hand away. If her body hadn't caved in with his touch, she would have taken the opportunity to sink her teeth into his fine tanned flesh. If her body hadn't been weak with wanting more, she would have scowled and scolded and stopped him. Instead, she fell into that cool pool of blue and her gasping lungs seemed to fill with water instead of oxygen. It took a moment or many before she reached for the edge, dragged her wet and bedraggled self out and growled in a tone of pure provoked bear. "Don't. Touch. Me."

His mouth tweaked at the corners and a wash of desire filled her—stirring her insides into a delicious spin. It coloured everything from the way he poured the wine, to the way he produced strawberries and fresh raspberries from the depths of his bag.

"They're organic." He picked up a plump, juicy raspberry and lifted it towards her mouth. She caught his eye and he thought better of it, throwing it into his own mouth instead.

Memories of his brother's rakish charm rose like a ghoul and snapped her out of whatever spell he'd cast with his wine and his touch and his berries. The reality check was like a shower of ice to the heat radiating from her centre.

"What makes you think you're the black sheep of the family? You went into law."

"Guilty as charged, your honour, but I don't want my children to grow up without their father because he's at work. I don't want to spend more time with my secretary than my wife. Or take advantage of a young receptionist because my life is dull beyond endurance."

Scarlet physically recoiled. "Your brother's behaviour was reprehensible."

"It was." His tone was cheerful, as if they weren't having a scathing discussion about his older brother. "He and I are not close." His gaze said a lot of things. For one, it said he didn't like what his brother had done. Nor did he take his brother's side, which was something. "Our father was never home. The pressure of his work took a toll on his health and his family, and I don't want that. I don't want success at the cost of everything that's important."

"You're very wise for a… twenty-nine-year-old man?"

"I sometimes feel like I'm fifty."

"Are you telling me that mop of hair isn't real? A toupee?" Scarlet pretended to be devastated. She blamed the wine. It ran through her veins like an aphrodisiac and where before she'd found him marginally attractive, she now found him devastatingly handsome. She didn't drink. With colleagues. Ever. She didn't do work functions. She especially didn't do end-of-year Christmas parties. Why had she thought a roadside picnic was any different? She had rules for a reason. Rules kept her safe. Rules kept her on task and focused on her goals. How had she let another Radcliff drive all sense from her head? She glanced at her wrist. PS. Pissed and Stupid. It was a message from her younger self, etched in indelible ink. She'd been charmed and wooed and weak. Never again would she feel like such a fool. She lowered her glass and reached for some berries, her gaze straying to the road. The quiet, empty road.

"What does it stand for?"

"Hmmm?" There were dandelions in the grass and the breeze

stirred them, so their feathery tops floated and fluttered.

"Your ink. You don't strike me as the kind of girl who gets a tattoo."

"PartnerShip." She'd answered without thinking and now she snapped her attention back to the man who set her heart fluttering like the roadside weeds.

"That's some dedication to a goal."

He lifted a berry towards her mouth. "Don't make me hurt you, Radcliff." She scowled, and he laughed.

"Tell me about your family." He lazed in the sun, confident in his million-dollar suit.

"My parents were both primary school teachers. Education and achievement were high priorities for them, but there was a lot of love, too."

"They must be very proud of you."

Scarlet took a sip of her wine. "They're proud of my work ethic."

"Why the partnership or perish attitude?"

"I want to succeed." She glanced up and saw the roadside assistance vehicle fast approaching. "Hallelujah." She struggled to her feet and slipped her heels back on.

"Why is it so important that you need an inked reminder?"

"I don't expect you to understand." She smoothed her skirt over her hips.

"Try me."

"It's nice of you to ask." She turned her attention to the tall mechanic who had extracted himself from his vehicle. "But I don't have to explain myself to you."

Tony's head spun with WTF? He couldn't be falling for her. He'd never truly *fallen* for a woman before. Not like this. Not like he'd leapt from the crest of a mammoth big wave and lost his grip entirely. Not like he'd been pummelled and smacked his head. She was as prickly as a pufferfish, but he saw the woman behind the cloud of animosity. He saw her vulnerability. Why did he care? Did he feel guilty on his brother's behalf? She was a close-out, a rip, a dangerous swell. He was crazy to contemplate what he was contemplating… but her violet grey eyes drew him like a storm brewing over the ocean. She was competent and clever, and sassy and smart.

Scarlet turned as if she'd sensed his gaze and he winked, loving the flick of barbed tail in her eyes. Yep. She wanted him, but she'd fight him all the way and what was he thinking? It was a path to professional suicide. Geoffrey's career had taken years to recover from the bombshell she'd pitched his way. Not that he hadn't deserved it.

Tony savoured the sunshine and the view. Scarlet looked just fine in a business suit. Corporate and sedate, yes, but ravishing and distracting also came to mind. He would be wise to give her a wide berth. An ocean-wide berth.

There was nothing wrong with looking.

There was nothing wrong with getting to know her. From his brother's perspective, Scarlet was Eve herself. Their fling had destroyed his family. Never mind that Scarlet was one of many. Never mind that his brother was a player not a stayer. He hoped that trait wasn't in his genes. He hoped the early dementia trait wasn't either. He chewed on his lip. Life was short. His mum's death last year from breast cancer had taught him that much. Internalised resentment wasn't healthy, and he didn't want that for his own wife.

"All done, Radcliff. It's time to get back to the real world."

"You didn't try the chocolate-dipped orange slices." He held the bag out for her.

"Tempting."

Her violet gaze met his and the connection made his heart zing. "And healthy. Dried orange. Dark chocolate."

"They sound too good to be true. Okay." She reached over and took a piece, and he waited while she tasted. "Mmmm. They're good."

He grinned and started packing up their picnic. She stood and he reached for the blanket and gave it a shake. He tucked it into the boot with the leftover food. "I'm ready when you are."

"Thanks for lunch. I enjoyed it." Her smile was soft, but her gaze was guarded.

*Thanks, Bro.* The one woman who might have interested him and his brother had stymied any chance he might have had. Damn, Geoffrey.

Scarlet's brow puckered and it seemed that even the thought of his brother was enough to put her off. "Oh, you're welcome." He liked it when she softened. He liked it when the violet in her eyes went from stormy to balmy to a different kind of stormy. The kind of stormy that left his body strung out, craving to touch, to taste, to linger…

"Let's get back to work." She opened the door on the driver's side.

"Yes, Ma'am." He lowered himself into the passenger seat and tried to keep his attention on the road. In truth, the woman beside him intrigued him. She didn't talk to fill the silence and he was surprised to find he felt comfortable with her. There was no second-guessing, no need to impress her. He'd probably fail anyway.

"Where do your mum and dad live?" Her gaze turned towards him for a brief moment.

The question hung between them while he struggled to sort

his words into a palatable answer. In the end, his promise of honesty won out. "My mum's not with us anymore and dad lives in our family home in Camberwell." With a full-time caregiver. "He's not very well."

"I'm sorry to hear that."

He could hear the compassion in her tone and every cell in his body armoured itself against her. He didn't want her sympathy and his feelings regarding his mother's death and his father's deteriorating health confused him. As a child and adolescent, he'd found his father formidable, distant and disagreeable, but at his mother's funeral, he'd watched the man crumple. For that alone, he loved him. For that alone, he dragged his body to the office and worked harder than he'd ever worked because time was short.

"What about yours?"

"They live in Ballarat on a small property. They grow their own vegetables and have a few calves that they raise and sell."

"How often do you see them?"

"Not as often as I'd like." He heard the weight in her words.

They sat in silence and Tony watched the rural scenery recede, replaced by industrial buildings at the fringe of the city. He hadn't expected to like her. He hadn't expected his body to react to hers the way it had. *There are plenty more fish in the sea.* Yep, he knew it. And he wasn't looking for a relationship. Not now. Not yet. But that image of his children on the beach? It sharpened and for the first time, he saw them clearly. Their blonde hair, their violet-blue eyes, their smiles, so like Scarlet's.

The phone rang in his pocket and he drew it out. "Hello?"

Think and speak of the devil. "Ant, your receptionist tells me you're out of the office. On your first day? I'm in the foyer. There's been a bit of an emergency with Dad."

"What happened?"

"He's had a fall. A nasty one. He's in surgery. They're not sure he's going to make it. How far off are you?"

His gaze connected with Scarlet's, before she looked away. "About five minutes."

"Great. I'll wait for you and we can go together." He paused, then added. "Who's we?"

"I've been out on a site visit." He took a deep breath. "With Scarlet O'Connor."

"You're kidding, right?" His brother's anger spat along the airwaves. "Back away slowly, mate. She's a ball-buster." She sure brought the crazy out in his brother.

"I'll see you soon." Tony hit the end button and tucked the phone back into his suit pocket. How much of that had Scarlet heard? "My dad's had a fall. He's in a bad way."

"Oh, no. I'm so sorry. I only caught the last part of the conversation. My mind was miles away." Her knuckles appeared white from the tightness of her grip on the steering wheel and his heart sank.

"I'm sorry you heard that." No need to elaborate.

"Do you need me to drop you at the hospital?"

"No, Geoffrey's waiting at the office, but if you could drop me in Collins St. that would be great."

"Sure." She glanced across at him, concern on her face, compassion in the violet depths of her eyes. They slowed for a red light and she closed the convertible roof, lowering the volume of the music.

His mother's death had sucked the life from his father, and he'd become even more frail, confused and lost. They'd resorted to telling him she'd gone to the shops. It helped to ease his suffering for a short time, but it didn't last. Tony's heart banged crazy-loud in his ears. All those lost years. He hadn't appreciated how precious they were. Grief, regret, pain pounded in his head. When they drew up in front of the office, Scarlet reached over and rested her hand on his arm.

"I hope your dad's okay." Her gaze held his, warm and comforting.

"Thanks, I appreciate it." His chest swelled and a wave of emotion swamped him.

"Ant." His brother's voice interrupted the moment. A hunted look flashed into Scarlet's eyes before the violet crystallised into hard black. No way had she been the one at fault.

Tony stepped out of the car and turned in time to see a twisted smile on his brother's face. "Scarlet O'fucking Connor."

"It's been a long time, Geoffrey." Scarlet's voice was calm and dignified.

"If you'll excuse us." Tony slammed the door and pushed his brother in the direction of his Audi, parked illegally in front of the building. "We need to go before we get towed away."

# Chapter Four

Scarlet seethed and cussed and accelerated just a little too fast as she turned the corner and headed towards the carpark. The wheels squealed in protest and echoed the sensation in every cell of her body. She'd relaxed her guard... with a Radcliff. And his older brother hadn't changed a bit. He was as arrogant as ever. But he'd aged and not well. She couldn't remember why she'd found him attractive. There had been pain, raw and real in the clear blue of Tony's eyes. He wasn't Geoffrey and his father was hurt.

She gathered her things from the back of the car and eyed her watch. Plenty of time before her three o'clock hearing. She forced herself into the lift and arrived with more of a sweat on her brow than if she'd taken the ten flights of stairs. She strode into her office and got back to work. She didn't think of Tony for the next four hours. Well, that was almost true. By the time she walked into the tearoom to refresh her water bottle the office was quiet. She preferred the office after five o'clock. The busy hum stopped, and she could focus on her work without interruption.

She was deep in the contents of a file, assessing the case and taking notes, when there was a knock on her door.

She looked up and saw Tony, his eyes the colour of Hobsons

Bay on a winter's day. He looked dishevelled, his tie loose and his hair mussed like he'd raked his hands through it. He looked done in. "How's your dad?"

"He didn't make it."

"Oh, no." Scarlet felt the force of it like a medicine ball to the chest. "I'm so sorry."

"It's a blessing in disguise. My dad was increasingly lost in time and he couldn't understand why my mum wasn't around. He was devastated by her death but confused. He thought she'd left him. God knows he gave her reason enough."

"Dementia?" She didn't want to feel anything for Tony Radcliff, but he looked so shattered and forlorn that she didn't have the heart to reject him the way she'd promised herself she would on the way back to her office. She nodded to the chair in front of her desk. "Do you want to come in."

"Sure." He collapsed into the soft leather bucket seat. "Thanks. It's been a tough day."

"I left your wine in your office."

"Thanks. This morning feels like a lifetime ago. I thought you would have gone home by now. It's past nine thirty."

"I needed to get this sorted for a mention tomorrow morning."

"There's so much pressure in this business. What of the cost? What of the pound of flesh that has to be sacrificed? Don't you question it? Don't you ever get angry?"

"No, I want to succeed. Badly." Her mother's warning echoed in her head and she felt the urge to cover her ears. There was plenty of time for a family *after* she'd achieved what she'd set out to achieve. She should thank Geoffrey Radcliff. He'd hardened her resolve—her goal was resolute and unyielding like hot metal thrust into cold water.

"I see that." He raked his hand through his hair and his bicep bulged under the sateen cotton of his shirt.

She shouldn't have noticed. She shouldn't have heated in response. She shouldn't have invited him into her office in the first place, but it seemed she had a thing for wounded wolves in one hundred percent fine wool. "Have you eaten?" She shouldn't have cared.

"No." His body straightened in his chair. "Have you?"

She shook her head. "But I have a packet of Tim Tams if you're interested." She pulled them out of her drawer and passed them across. "Here."

"Chocolate biscuits? You're a life saver. I'll make some tea to go with them. Would you like one?"

"Sure. I'd love a green tea." No, she scolded. No, thank you. I'm working. Her words weren't cooperating. Her body wasn't cooperating. And when she turned her attention back to the file on her desk, she'd lost her flow and instead of her mind feeling focused, it was infused with syrupy warmth. It had been so long since she'd felt anything but cold determination, she found it surprising and addictive. You're nearly done. Push through. Another ten minutes. She'd just finished when Tony lowered a mug of tea onto her desk. A mug. Clearly, tea etiquette hadn't rated highly in his expensive private school education.

"Sorry about the mug. The cups were in the dishwasher."

Or maybe she was wrong. "That's okay." She expected scalding, but he'd put a dash of cold water in just how she liked it. "Thanks." Thoughtful. In the middle of his distress, he'd been thoughtful. It threw her. The same way he'd thrown her all day. And he'd lost his father. Grief was there in the slump of his shoulders and her heart refused to stay frozen. His father. She couldn't bear the thought of losing her own. It would be like having her heart ripped from her chest.

"I should have made it for *you*. I'm so sorry for your loss." The formality of the words echoed in her head and she swallowed them along with a sip of her tea. She was rusty at the friend-thing. She kept people at a safe distance, but Tony wouldn't stay put. He didn't fit the lawyer mould. He didn't fit the Radcliff mould. He threw her and that's what had her in a tailspin.

"It's funny. I miss him already and it really hurts, but in truth, it was only when my mum died last year that I connected with him. He wasn't an affectionate man. I realise now, he showed his love differently. He showed it by pushing himself to be better. By working hard to succeed. By providing for his family. I didn't get it." He reached for a Tim Tam and dunked it into his tea.

Her father did that with Tim Tams, too. They were *his* favourite and *her* go-to comfort food.

"There are lots of different kinds of love…" She took a biscuit and carefully dunked it into her tea. She savoured the hot sweetness and when she caught Tony's eye, she smiled. "…I guess some kinds are harder to recognise than others."

"Yes." Tears welled in his eyes and pain flashed across his face.

Oh, hell. She was making it worse. "I'm sorry. I'm sure he was proud of you." She pushed a box of tissues towards him.

"I don't know. He never said. That wasn't his way." Tony took a tissue and blew his nose. Her body reacted to his closeness. He smelt musky and male, and there was a slight citrus scent beneath the rest.

"What about your mum?" Scarlet dunked the other end of her biscuit into her tea. She didn't like floating biscuit crumbs so two dunks per biscuit was her limit.

"She, too, struggled to live up to dad's expectations. He was demanding and critical and hard to live with, but he loved her. I guess she loved him back or she wouldn't have put up with him for all those years." Tony settled back into his seat and picked up his mug, blowing across the hot liquid.

"When's the funeral?"

"No date yet, but within the week. My brother will want to organise it. It doesn't matter how old I am, I'll always be the baby of the family and in his eyes, less competent."

"Is that why you want the partnership position? To prove yourself to Geoffrey?" Scarlet reached for another biscuit. She hadn't realised she was hungry.

"Partnership is the only thing that will earn his respect."

"And his respect is important to you?"

"Self-respect is important to me." Tony's wet eyes met hers.

"I get it." He finished his biscuit and took a gulp of his tea. His face was strained, his eyes cloudy and distant, like his thoughts were far away.

"Are you nearly done for the day?" he asked, his voice quiet.

"Yes." She sipped her tea, grateful for the warm comfort of it.

"I'm going for a ride down to Torquay. Would you like to join me?" His words were casual, but his gaze arrowed deep inside her.

"Now?"

"Yes. I want to stand in the ocean and feel the waves. I want to see the moon and the stars."

"I'm tired. It's been a long day." *Go*, a small voice inside her whispered. *Are you crazy?* "Did you say ride? What are we talking?"

"A Suzuki GSX R 1300. I thought you'd like the power of it. Another time." He took a generous gulp of his tea.

"I'm not dressed for it, Radcliff."

"You can wear my one-piece and I'll wear my leather jacket

and jeans. They're in my locker downstairs. I've got a spare helmet."

The sadness in his gaze pulled at her. Damn. Where was denial when she needed it? *Go home, Scarlet.* The thought of her bed beckoned, and she stifled a yawn.

"You look tired. You've had a tough day." His gaze held hers, and now that it was gone, she missed the mischievous sparkle in his eyes.

"Your day was worse."

"Yep." He drained his mug and stood. "I'll see you tomorrow. After eight thirty." He grinned and the sad power of it punched her in the midriff, her resistance crumbling like her Tim Tam had softened in her hot tea.

"Radcliff?"

He turned from the doorway and magic seemed to shimmer between them. "Fine, I could do with some fresh air."

"Really?" His face lit up and his eyes lost their wintry hue.

Hell. She'd live to regret this, but she couldn't bear the defeat that hung over him like a grey fog. "Give me ten minutes. I'll meet you downstairs."

The door to the stairway slammed and Scarlet appeared in the locker room, her bag over her shoulder. Grief had Tony by the throat and misery weighed on him like thick sludge.

"Are you sure you wouldn't prefer to be alone?" She dropped her leather tote bag on the bench beside him and sat, her eyes filled with a compassion he didn't deserve.

"I'd like your company, but it's fine if you'd rather go home. I can see how tired you are." She looked drained and he had no doubt she'd worked all weekend as well. His stomach tightened and squeezed, and he feared she might take the out. He wouldn't blame her. But the thought of Scarlet's arms wrapped around him was better than the yawning loneliness that threatened to devour him. His parents were gone. Both of them.

"I'm good."

"I really appreciate it." This was about compassion. Hers. And it said more about the woman she was, than the man he was. But he'd take it. He handed over his one-piece leather outfit. "It might be a bit loose, but…"

"It's something between me and the bitumen. I get it. I've got runners somewhere, too." She riffled through her bag.

"You can trust me, Scarlet."

Her eyebrows lifted, her eyes lit with mauves and blues, and she smiled, soft and slow. "We'll see about that."

She turned and disappeared into a change room. He pulled his leather jacket on, and hung his suit on a hanger in his locker. The night was warm, and he couldn't wait to get out on the M1. He tucked his wallet into the inside pocket of his jacket and zipped it up. He reached for his helmet.

"What do you think?"

Scarlet in a business suit was a knock-out. Scarlet in bike leathers? His heart banged against his ribcage like he'd hit the road at speed and his body skidded out of control. The kerthunk when he finally got it together roared in his ears. Scarlet was sacred ground and he had no right thinking what he was thinking. He swallowed against the raspy territory of his throat and when his words finally found their way through, they were as dry as a crisp. "You look good."

He passed over a helmet and led the way to the carpark where his black Suzuki GSX R 1300 rested against its stand. He straddled it before pulling it upright. "All aboard."

She stood back and checked it out. "A Suzuki Hayabusa?"

"You know bikes? Have you been on one before?"

"Yes, but not often. It's a four-cylinder. How fast can it go?"

"It's the fastest thing on two wheels. You're gonna need to put your arms around my waist and lean with the bike."

"Got it." Scarlet settled herself on the back and wrapped her arms around him. Her body pressed against him, close, so close. And his insides thrummed. She was what he'd needed all along. Her warm embrace soothed the hurt. The revving motor soothed the restlessness. And the acceleration through the warm night air soothed his heart. Traffic lights slowed them down, but once they were on the M1, they reached the one hundred kilometre-per-hour speed limit in moments. The bike throbbed beneath them and inside his helmet, the tears he hadn't cried were blasted away by the press of the night air. Sobs rose with every deep, long breath. His father was gone. It was a blessing. He knew it. His father had been on a slippery slope to nowhere good. Losing the faculty of his mind was a cruel betrayal to a man who had prided himself on his superior intelligence. The white lines flashed before him, the beam of his headlight carving a bright path through the darkness.

The warm press of Scarlet's body against him dragged at his attention. He liked her there. He more than liked her there. With her close, the pain of his father's passing was bearable. With her close, the choking weight in his chest lifted and that awful sensation of being dumped by a powerful wave settled. Air filled his lungs. Relief filled his heart. It would be okay. It was okay. It was better than okay. With every kilometre, with every shadowy tree they passed, he felt stronger.

Scarlet's helmet banged against his and he wondered if she'd fallen asleep. She was exhausted, yet she'd put his needs before her own. Why?

She should hate him.

She did hate him.

She'd pushed him away at every opportunity, yet here she was with the younger brother of the man who'd treated her so badly. Her strength of character was formidable, and she impressed him again for the thousandth time that day.

He didn't mix business with pleasure. He prided himself on that. Weak men had tawdry office affairs. Weak men like his brother and his father. Not him. He'd never felt the need. In hindsight, he'd never been tempted.

*Scarlet was temptation in capital letters.*

Scarlet had trusted him enough to get on the back of his bike. Enough to join him in this not-well-thought-out escapade. Enough to be with him on an empty beach. In the dark. Alone.

No way would he take advantage of that.

# Chapter Five

Scarlet had never straddled such a beast of a bike before. It throbbed beneath her and devoured the road like a half-starved wildcat. With her arms wrapped tightly around Tony's hard stomach and her body pressed intimately against his rounded back, she quivered with a trillion tiny tremors in places she'd forgotten existed. The air pushed against them, warm and lovely and the night held the promise of secrecy, the shield of darkness. She closed her eyes to better savour the sensory storm, her chin against Tony's shoulder. When had she experienced anything this blissful? She wanted to believe that the throbbing ache in her centre had more to do with the bike and less to do with the man—the bike was a very fine specimen and there was something to be said for a powerful engine—but it was Tony who brought her body to life.

*His father has just died*, she chided herself. *He's full to the brim with the pain of it and your mind is going to places it shouldn't.* Her heart expanded and filled with compassion. His humanness appealed to her more than the rest. He'd shown his feelings. He'd promised honesty and he'd given her that. And she found she liked it. She liked it a lot. He hadn't pretended he was fine. He hadn't belittled or denied his feelings. *He's a Radcliff*, she warned. *The black sheep of the family*, she countered.

She held him tighter and opened herself to the freedom of their flight through the night.

The drop in the high-pitched yowl of the motor and the forward thrust of her position on the seat alerted her to their arrival. Tony pulled into a car park in front of the foreshore and cut the engine. The silence rang in her ears and they sat motionless for a long moment observing the full moon over the water, the foamy heads of the waves caught in its silvery path. Tony rested his hand on her knee and her body reacted like a lit fuse. When Tony flicked out the stand and tipped the bike slightly to one side, her foot reached the ground and she pulled her other leg free. It took a moment to find her land legs but by the time she'd removed her gloves and helmet and looped it over the handlebars, he was there beside her.

"Come."

He took her hand in his and dragged her towards the sand and the water. He could have let her hand go. She could have pulled free. But, instead, the press of his palm against hers stirred all kinds of trouble in her body. She kicked off her runners and her toes curled in the cool silk of the sand. It was like every sense was on steroids. Loud and hard to ignore. They walked in silence, listening to the pounding thud of the waves against the shore and the soothing hiss of the water as it rushed forward and pulled back.

"This is beautiful."

"It is." His in-breath was audible. "And so are you." He turned her towards him and with his free hand pushed a wayward strand of her hair back from her face. "Thank you for coming with me. Thank you for trusting me. I'm glad I'm not alone."

Scarlet's heart thudded and pounded in her chest. More intimate waves thudded and pounded through her body. Tony's eyes looked dark in the monochromatic light, but she could tell from the tilt of his head that he studied her. Who knew what he saw reflected in her eyes? Their trip on the motorbike had been like foreplay. Pure and potent. Desire roared in her ears and danced on her tongue. Her pulse banged, unruly and wild. Adrenaline rushed through her veins. Abandon, too. There was the magnetic pull of his mouth. The plush promise of his lips. The hunger he stirred within her.

"We're not going there, Scarlet." His voice was ragged and abrasive. "I'm not my brother. I will not take advantage of your compassion. Your kindness. Let's walk before I kiss you."

"What if I want you to kiss me." The words were out there, between them. Her whole body convulsed. What had she done?

"You don't want that."

Her step faltered. "I think I might."

He wrapped his arm around her shoulders and pulled her close, but he propelled them forward, his feet kicking up the sand. "Let's walk."

Scarlet relaxed into the heat of him. He reached over and kissed her forehead. Chaste. Friendly. And she was relieved. She was embarrassed, too. She'd as good as propositioned him and he'd as good as said, no. Awkward. But awkward wasn't how she felt when he drew her close. She felt protected. Coveted. Safe.

The waves—inside and out—curved and crashed and pounded and pulled. The night whispered around them and it was like they were the only two people on the planet, along with the billions and trillions of stars that looked down upon them. A vast wonderland of sparkling diamonds.

"I like to think the stars are the souls of those who have gone before us, shining down from heaven. Do you see the Southern

Cross? There." He held her close and pointed upwards. She followed the line of his arm and nodded, her body in meltdown. "Do you see the brightest star in the Southern Cross? It's called the Acrux. I like to think it's my mum, and look… do you see the shiny one beside it? My father is with her. Two stars sparkling with love."

Scarlet grappled with her throat muscles. "You came here to feel closer to your mum and dad?"

"Crazy, right?"

He pulled her close, and his warmth and strength seeped into her bones.

"The stars are way clearer here than in the city." His voice was low and husky and resonated like a soft stroke over sensitive skin. "This is the beach where I came as a child. My mate's holiday house is over there. It came on the market a few years ago."

"Did you buy it?"

He nodded. "I did."

"Is this where you live? You travel into the city every day?" The thought took her down like a rogue wave.

"Yep. Most days. My parents have an apartment in Spencer St., and I stay there if I'm too tired to make the trip." He paused, his gaze on hers. "Thanks for today. It turns out I like spending time with you."

Her heartbeat galloped in her chest, wild and white-eyed. "I like spending time with you, too, against my better judgement."

"I'm sorry for what my brother did."

"It wasn't your fault." The words echoed in her ears. She could hardly blame Tony for his brother's behaviour or let that colour her opinion of him.

"I'm not like Geoffrey."

"No, you're not." She turned into his embrace, pressed herself against him and tilted her face upwards. His big hands settled on her hips before exploring her back. They pulled her closer and he held her tight. She felt safe. Foolishly safe. Stupidly safe, but there was nothing safe about the way his mouth lowered towards hers, then retreated, his gaze seeking the night sky. She curled her hand around the nape of his neck, pulled his mouth back towards hers, closed the gap. His lips were velvety soft—she kissed him, a soft, gentle coaxing, and when he invited space between them and went to speak, she closed the gap again. This time he didn't hesitate. This time he feasted and when his tongue took hers in a sultry tango, she melted into him, her eyes closed, her hand lost in the thick, silky softness of his hair, her ears loud with the thunder of her pulse. He tasted—delicious—and with every thrust of his tongue, every smooth, tantalising stroke, her centre stormed and calmed. He held her reverently. His mouth worshipped hers. He loosened her hair and combed it back with his fingers, his touch careful and magical.

Scarlet didn't know how long they stood there, wrapped together, their bodies humming with shared passion, but the harsh cry of a gull startled her from the lulling beauty of it.

She stepped back, her mind reeling. What had she done? "I'm sorry."

"I'm not..." His gaze held hers.

There was hurt there. From her apology? She wrapped her arms around herself and pulled away. The surreal perfection of the night swam before her eyes.

"...unless you kissed me out of pity."

"No." She shook her head, her emotions raw. "If anyone was in need of a pity kiss, that would be me."

"What do you mean?"

"I don't remember the last time I came to the beach. Or saw a night sky that wasn't bleached by the city lights through eyes that weren't blurred from overwork." Or the last time she'd kissed a man and felt it—like tectonic plates colliding.

"It's easy to get caught up in the rat-race. My brother did it. My father did it. I saw what it did to my mother. To my brother's marriage."

"My parents never allowed work to get in the way of family."

"But achievement and education were important to them," said Tony. "Maybe you became over-focused on those things and took the rest for granted."

"Maybe you're right. I don't remember the last time I had fun." She swiped her face. Tears? She was grateful for the darkness.

"Let's go for a swim?"

"I didn't bring bathers."

"You don't need them." His teeth flashed in the moonlight.

"Skinny dipping? Are you asking me to get naked with you?" Scarlet's body was a hive of don't-do-it, do-it, no-I-can't, yes-you-can, are-you-out-of-your-mind?

"If you want to."

"You really are a Radcliff."

"I can't help my genes, but I promise I won't take advantage of you." He raked a hand through his hair and his eyes bored into hers. The air snapped with electric currents, the dangerous wattage frying her nerve endings and cranking her inside temperature to boiling.

"Unless you want me to."

The blood stopped in her veins. Her thoughts collided—collected themselves. "I bet you're used to women throwing themselves at you." That was a splash of cold ocean on hot skin. The motor bike ride. His house conveniently a stone's throw away. His bed. Her body puckered and pulled, and her stomach tied itself in knots.

"Not your kind of woman... no."

He was a player. She wasn't?

"Scarlet, we're not talking about sex here. We're talking about having fun, letting go a little. The water—the darkness—will protect your modesty."

"The last time a Radcliff said something like that, I ended up in a locked lift compartment with no way to escape."

"My brother did that?"

"Your brother is a very driven kind of guy and he wasn't going to let a little thing like consent get in the way of achieving his goal. If I hadn't panicked, he wouldn't have gotten as far as he did but... I'm not as weak as I look."

"I'm not my brother. Or my father." His eyes glistened in the darkness. "And you're far from weak."

Oh, hell. His father. Now, she'd upset him and those barriers around her heart? They collapsed like a sandcastle before a wave. She should say no. The trouble was... she didn't want to say no. *You want to have sex with him?* Yes. She wanted to have sex with him. In the waves. She wanted to orgasm with the wind in her hair, and her scream lost in the crash and the splash of the water. No. She didn't. She was far from weak... usually. "I kissed you."

"I kissed you back."

"I liked it."

"So, did I. Let's go for a swim but keep your underwear on. I'm only human and you're a beautiful woman."

He started to peel off his leather jacket and dropped each item of clothing in a pile on the sand. The damn moon shone bright—full and silvery in the night. Scarlet stood mesmerised, unable to drag her eyes away. He was muscular. Ripped. It was like she'd been dragged into the sea and her mouth grappled for oxygen. Dizzy. Her head spun. The sight of his body stole her breath.

"Come on. What are you waiting for? I'm going in."

His briefs were black and as sexy as sin. His bum was tight, his legs were long, and his shoulders were broad. His grin was infectious, and his frivolous joy was even more so. He splashed into the shallows, his feet spraying water everywhere.

They didn't have a towel was her last lucid thought before she stripped. What the hell was she doing? He'd come into her day like a freaking cyclone, leaving her in a naked spin. An almost naked spin, she thought, as she dropped the motorcycle suit, peeled out of her shirt and followed him into the waves in her black briefs and bra.

He dived under the waves and surfaced right beside her, picking her up and throwing her backwards into the sea like she weighed less than a piece of driftwood. She gulped a mouthful of air before disappearing under the wave. She grappled to find her feet, pounded by the surf. She surged back into the air, gulping and laughing. His arms wrapped around her and the skin-on-skin feel of him roared in her ears like a supersonic jet. Their mouths locked. The waves buffeted their bodies, but they were stronger together than they were apart.

He tasted of salt and freedom and her body was as exhilarated by his kiss as their jaunt on the open road. She was aware of him, hard and eager against her, and the thundering roar of the ocean echoed inside her. She wanted him. She wanted him with a passion she'd never experienced before. She wanted to throw caution to the wind and take him inside her where she burned and squirmed and craved his touch. Their kiss became more frantic, more raw, more demanding. She pressed herself against the rough hair of his legs, the hard ridge of his arousal. She moved in sync with the thrust of his tongue. Her body wept with desire. His groan resonated inside her and his pain was hers.

She wrapped herself closer and her body roared. All her focus was on his mouth and the feel of him against her, the rising storm within her.

"You're killing me," he groaned, and she begged—she wasn't proud of it—she begged him to bury himself inside of her.

"I've got nothing, Scarlet. And a promise is a promise."

She kissed him harder. He cared enough to think of protection? To keep his promise. She kissed him with enough force to bruise and her frustration rose until she thought she'd die from the emptiness inside her… "Doesn't matter," she groaned. "I take birth control pills. Heavy periods." Too much information. The thought pulled her back for a moment, but the tide of sensation in her body would not be denied. The pain of it was too intense. The pleasure too agonising. "For Christ's sake, Radcliff. Do it already and hurry up."

"I promised." If the waves hadn't splashed about them and salty droplets hadn't hung from their eyelashes, she would have seen the tears in his eyes.

"I relieve you from your promise. I swear to God, Radcliff. You started this; you need to finish it." He pulled no punches. His hands grappled with their wet underwear until she was naked, and so was he. He scooped her up by the buttocks and she wrapped her legs around him, leveraging herself higher. One thrust and he filled her. Joined with her until she moved against him and soared with the joy of it. Her hands clung to his biceps, his shoulders, his lats... a sensory feasting that was lost in the sensory storm he whipped up in her body. The waves crashed around them, but he stood strong and valiant, while she rode him like a V8 engine, driving them both beyond endurance until her cries echoed with the waves and his orgasm pounded inside her. She sagged against him, the aftershocks of their coupling driving more yelps from her lips. He pulled her close and she kissed his neck, his ears, his wet face.

"Holy moly," she muttered, and he laughed, a deep vibration that nearly sent her over the edge again.

"You could say that." His breath was short and frantic, and his heart banged against hers. "Lucky I'm young. I don't think an older man would have survived that." He nuzzled her neck. "How do you stay this trim and delicious when you spend so many hours at the office. Your bum is outstanding."

She giggled, the laughter bubbling up from deep inside. "I take the stairs a lot. Ten flights of them. Carrying files. A full workout."

"Because of my brother and what happened?"

"Partly. I don't like enclosed spaces, especially lifts." And it was then that she realised she hadn't felt the usual panic when she got up close and personal with a man. This man was open space. The vastness of the ocean. The night sky. The open road. Not once had she felt closed in or afraid. Her body had opened to him, too. Readily. Willingly. Wantonly.

She lowered her mouth to his and together they tasted, their kiss more intimate, more tender than it was before. "How are your legs?" She suddenly realised he was holding her weight and she was wrapped around him like an ocean vine.

"Fine." He paused. "Getting tired."

The laughter gurgled up again. "You're doing all the work."

"Trust me. This is not my idea of work. If it was… I'd be a workaholic like you."

Scarlet eased herself off him, crying out when they separated, the rush of the salt water cold after the heat of his body. He pulled her close and they stood together, their arms wrapped around each other, the light of the moon shimmering on the foaming, frothing, fizz of the water.

"Where's our underwear?"

"I haven't a clue."

"You threw them away?"

"Honey, you were in a hurry." He chuckled. "But I kind of like the feel of you naked against me."

"You feel pretty good yourself, but you did look sexy in your black jocks." The ocean churned and surged around them, completely devoid of their clothing.

"You look sexy in whatever you wear."

Scarlet held on like she, too, might disappear into the night. "Even compromised principles?"

"Especially compromised principles." His tone was jovial, but his gaze was serious as he took her chin in his hands. "Tell me you're not going to regret this."

"How could I?" She leant forward to press her lips softly against his. "I enjoyed it too much."

He answered in kind, murmuring, "I'll remind you of that tomorrow in the harsh light of the day."

"Are you going to invite me into your place for a hot shower?"

"After I dunk you a few more times."

Scarlet felt his hands around her and she sailed through the air, landing hard on the back of a wave. The water engulfed her, and she flailed about with her arms and legs. It seemed like forever before she felt his strong arms grip her and drag her to the surface. She coughed and spluttered, and struggled to catch her breath. "Are you trying to get rid of the competition, Radcliff?"

"I'm kind of partial to the competition. What happened?" He drew her close against the hard planes of his body, and she savoured the feel of him against her. Skin to skin.

"I got disoriented." She shivered as a breeze blew over them.

"Let's get you into a hot shower and I'll make you a hot chocolate, extra marshmallows. You're cold."

"How are we supposed to get to your house?" Her teeth chattered and banged against each other. "What if the neighbours are awake?"

"There're mostly retired folk around here. They've probably been asleep for a while."

"Let's hope so." Scarlet pulled herself out of his arms and surged from the water in a full run, her laughter skipping ahead of her. She caught sight of her black bra washed up on the sand and deviated back to grab it. "Look what I found!"

"And look what I've got," he countered, and she grinned when she saw his sexy black jocks and her own black knickers. "You're quite the fisherman."

"And you're quite the mermaid."

Tony stirred the organic chocolate mix into a mug and waited for the kettle to boil. His small beach shack was deceptive. The inside was recently renovated and had all the latest finishes and appliances, while the outside retained its humble, weather-beaten appearance except for the new guttering. He was tempted to join Scarlet in the shower, but he was worried about how she'd feel when she came down from her sensory high.

Goodness knows his own body was still weak from the explosive crazy of their sexual encounter. It had been just the right antidote to the emotions that stormed inside him. It had been one hell of a day. He was exhausted. It was a work night after all. He put out some cinnamon cake. It was his mum's recipe and he'd taken to making it after she died. Funny how the taste and smell of it brought his memories of her back to life.

He tightened the towel around his hips and had just taken a bite when Scarlet came into the room drying her hair with a towel. She wore one of his old t-shirts and it was long enough to look like a dress.

"How are you feeling?"

"Exhilarated. Exhausted. You?"

"Same."

Her eyes glowed like amethyst and her smile gave him chills all over. She settled herself at his island bench. "Nice marble." She ran her hands over it and smiled.

"Here." He pushed the cup towards her and cut another piece of cake. He put it onto a plate for her with a small fork.

"Did you make this?"

"Life isn't all about work." Her eyes looked huge in her freshly washed face, and her skin was clear and pale. His heart hammered in his chest and he couldn't quite believe she was here in his kitchen.

"The motorbike ride sure wasn't a hardship." She took a sip of her drink, her eyes closing to savour the sweetness.

Tony felt a jolt in his midriff. "Thank you for tonight." The words seemed paltry compared with the sentiment behind them. "Today was tough, but you made tonight special. Something good to remember. Something to offset the sad."

"You're making it sound like a one-off." Her eyes snapped open and the violet shadows were back.

"Oh, I want to do it again, but I know things will change when we get back to the office." Scarlet's gaze held his and his stomach clenched. Her hair was wet and pushed back from her face. The force of his attraction sucker-punched him in the belly. Blue blazes. He loved her in his t-shirt. He loved watching her eat cake. Every slide of the fork from her delectable mouth stirred him mercilessly and ratcheted up the tension in his body. Her lips were rosy, even without lipstick. She smiled at him. A soft, secret smile so potent, it nearly floored him with desire. He sipped his hot chocolate and fought the flames that ravaged him. His body was hard. So ready. So hungry for hers.

"I'm going to take a shower." He tightened the towel around his hips and turned away.

"Better make that a cold one, Radcliff."

He turned and her smile was radiant. Heat flared and his blood ran south. "Wicked woman..."

"Ah, but I'm not from the West."

He couldn't stop the curiosity. "Where *do* you live?"

"In Middle Park. In a terrace house."

"I pictured you in a high-rise city apartment." Lording it over the world, although first impressions weren't always correct. He glanced at the clock on the living room wall. It was well past midnight. A lot had changed over the course of a day. For one, he now knew she disliked lifts and there was little chance she'd live in a high-rise city apartment. For two, she wasn't the woman he'd thought she was. She was far from the ice queen of yesterday morning.

"Would you like me to take you home? Or would you rather sleep here, and I'll drop you home in the morning? I have a guest room, or you could sleep with me." He said it easily enough, but the thought of her in his bed, her blonde hair spread across the silver of his sheets, the moonlight catching her skin took those flames and raised them a thousand degrees.

"Sleep?" Her eyebrows rose.

She was onto him. "I'll go and have a shower while you work out what you'd like to do." He turned and realised he liked the look of her in his kitchen. He liked a lot of things about her. Like how she was driven and competent. And her fetish for V8 motors. And how she melted beneath his touch, her heat, her hunger... and *that* made walking even more difficult.

He turned the faucet, closed his eyes and tipped his face into the warmth of the hot spray. His mind was on Scarlet, her incredible responsiveness, the way she cried when she climaxed, the way her lips moulded to his, the way her arms encircled his body. Had he conjured her from the sheer intensity of his desire for her?

"Let's not waste that enthusiasm you've got going there, Radcliff." Scarlet. Naked. Behind him. She reached for the soap and slid it over his torso and down to where he jerked into rapacious life. "Wicked woman."

"So, you said."

Her mouth was on his neck and his brain short-circuited. His blood had long left his head, and he was past reasoning. He was past promising or worrying or even thought. When he could stand it no longer, he turned, and his body collided with hers sending his circuitry into overload. "Hand over the soap, O'Connor."

"Pushy."

He gently prised the soap from her hand. She slid against him and the feel of her body was... he clamped his lips to hers and tasted like she was his last meal. Never before had he become so lost in a woman that he didn't know which way was up, like being dumped by a killer wave.

He ran the soap over her body, lathering her up until her sexy curves were slick and the soap dropped to the floor with a thud. His sudsy touch lingered on the full deliciousness of her buttocks. Her nipples brushed, silky and pebble-hard, against his chest, and she groaned into his lips. His arousal throbbed against the softness of her stomach and he stepped her back until she leaned against the tiled wall, his kiss deepening, his tongue lashing hers. She wrapped her arms around his neck, her breasts swollen, the hard peaks provocative, and devoured him right back, her mouth bruising, her teeth grazing. Her body writhed and slipped against his and stirred him into a frenzy. When her hand reached down to explore him, he near blew from the thrill of it and when she pushed them back under the water and positioned herself just so, he sank into her velvety heat. Her cry rang in his ears and her legs wrapped around his waist, drawing him deeper and driving him beyond thought. He supported her with his hands, and she rode him until her body convulsed around him and he couldn't hold back any longer.

He struggled for breath and his blood thundered in his ears. Sweet mercy. The woman was wild. She clung to him, her hot breath on his neck, her chest banging against his with the force of her heartbeat. He gasped for air, his chest heaving, his breath short. "Wow."

"Wow."

Her laugh gurgled into his neck before her mouth moved to his. Her tasting was smooth and soft and quiet—like the bay in the early morning. He sank into it. Slowly. Settling. And with it came peace. His eyes closed. The storm in his body eased. And he found something he hadn't known he was missing.

# Chapter Six

Sunlight struck Scarlet's face. She cringed and lifted her hand to cover her eyes. Her body ached and she could barely lift her head.

"Rise and shine."

She opened one eye against the punishment of the light and saw Tony, his hair wet, his wetsuit peeled down to his waist. His chest was tanned and firm and delicious. His arms were tanned and firm and delicious. "You've been for a surf."

"A quick one." He winked and there were those dimples. They reached out and pulled at her senses.

"We need to get you home and we need to get to work."

"Oh my God. What day is it?" Where was she? Who was she?

"Tuesday." He grinned and it sucker punched her in the midriff, stealing her breath.

"Coffee?" He held out a cup and the aroma penetrated her stupor.

She reached out for it like a woman drowning. "Bless you." She took a sip and the shroud of exhaustion lifted. Another and she was able to open both eyes. A third and she leapt from the bed. "I need a shower. Got to get going. What time is it?"

"Six."

"Six? It feels like the middle of the night."

"I can have you home by seven thirty if you move."

"Great. Thanks." She resisted the temptation of the delicious man and headed straight for the bathroom. She flicked the faucet and stood under the hot spray, her mind numb for long minutes until it turned to clothes and underwear—wet underwear—and oh hell, then it all came back. The ocean. The shower. The bed. No wonder her body felt like it had been hit by a tsunami.

"There's a hot towel here. And your underwear. Straight out of the dryer. I've topped up your coffee. Move, O'Connor. We need to go. There's toast, too."

"Thanks." The word near choked her. She was in Tony Radcliff's shower and it was all so comfortable and normal and easy. They'd had sex. They'd had more than sex. Scarlet wouldn't soon forget what had passed between them. Oh, hell. What had she done? *It's fine. You'll be fine. We'll be fine.*

She lifted the warm towel to her nose and pressed it close. It smelt fresh and clean and there was an undertone of citrus... orange.

She had to move. Her limbs were heavy, and her mind resisted the urge to rush. She rubbed the towel over her body and reached for her underwear. He'd left deodorant out for her and a new toothbrush. He knew his way into a woman's heart. He'd dried her underwear. Warmth flushed through her. Damn it. Why did he have to be so nice? It was hard to find fault. It was hard to find anything to use against him. She needed it. She needed to armour up. She needed to move. She glanced at her watch.

Her shirt barely covered her private parts. Where were the leathers she'd worn last night? Not in the bathroom. She'd have to saunter into the kitchen with her legs on display. It wasn't like he hadn't seen them already. It wasn't like he hadn't seen a lot more than her legs and when it came down to it, if she remembered correctly, it wasn't like her parts were that private anymore. Her cheeks heated and flushed pink in the mirror. It was a bit late for that.

Tony waited in front of Scarlet's two-story terrace house. The veranda had black and white tessellated tiles and the garden was manicured to perfection. It was quaint and beautiful and as precise as she was. She took the promised five minutes and not a moment longer and returned with a backpack full of clothes. He watched as she secreted the spare key away in a key lock. She straddled the bike and wrapped her arms around him. Where before his body had buzzed like a hive when she'd pressed against him, now her touch triggered a very intimate kind of reaction.

"Let's go," she prompted.

"One moment." His tone was guttural, his voice like a growl in the back of his throat. He forced his focus on to anything except the warmth of her arms around his midriff and the press of her body against his buttocks. He mastered the flames, pushed them back, took a deep breath. "Right."

The trip into the city was quick. He pulled in next to her car and cut the engine. He waited for Scarlet to dismount before he pulled off his helmet and with the bike on its stand, swung his leg over. Maybe it was her silence or the way the air tightened against his skin, but he sensed something was wrong. "What is it?"

"Look."

Someone had scratched the word SLUT into the shiny black duco of her door and worse, in big letters across the bonnet. She stood paralysed, like she'd been struck. "Why? Why would someone do that?"

"We left it here overnight. Maybe it was a random attack." No one could know what had happened between them. It made no sense. "I'll check in with Bob. See if there's anything on the security cameras." He took her into his arms and held her, but she didn't melt into him the way she had that morning. Instead, she stiffened and stepped away.

"You go and get changed. I'll speak with Bob. It's my problem."

"It's our problem. It was because of me your car was here overnight."

"That was my choice, Radcliff."

He could feel her pulling away, hardening, closing him out and he didn't like it. He wanted her back in his arms, hot and sensuous. He felt it, too. Cold, sharp reality. "Scarlet."

"See you upstairs."

"Okay." Of all the words they had to scratch into her car. There must be tens of dozens of cuss words they could have used, but no, they had to use the one word that was sure to hurt her the most. What had passed between them couldn't have been further from a meaningless fling. He'd felt a connection with her. A connection he hadn't felt with any other woman before. Maybe because his emotions were so raw after his father's death. Maybe because of what his brother had put her through. Maybe because she fitted against him like she was made to be there. *Snap out of it, Ant.* The word made his skin crawl. *She's a colleague. A lawyer, with goals and aspirations that clash with your own.*

May the best man—or woman—win. His own words echoed in his head. They could keep their work and personal lives separate, couldn't they?

He wanted to see her outside of work. He wanted more. He

wanted more than one incredible night. There was no doubt in his mind. One taste was not enough. Not nearly enough.

Scarlet stood by her car with tears in her eyes. The words scratched into the shiny black duco couldn't have hurt her more if they'd been etched into her own skin. And somewhere deep inside, they were. The echo of Geoffrey's accusation in the small, enclosed lift space rang in her ears. What was it about the Radcliff family? She'd behaved impeccably for a decade and after one day—one day—in Tony's company, she'd ignored the rules that had kept her safe and allowed herself one night—one night—of freedom. She eyed the word on the bonnet of her car. It hadn't felt that way. It had felt... special. They'd connected at a deeper level. She felt like she'd known him for years. He was fresh air to the stale her life had become. She was twenty-nine years old. Old enough to have a physical relationship with a man if it felt right. She wasn't a gullible nineteen-year-old anymore. She'd made the decision to be with Tony. She'd decided to have sex. They'd had sex on her terms. No stolen kisses in dark corners. They'd kissed in the open air. On the beach. And more. So much more.

*That's rubbish. You know his type. You're deluded if you think there's more to this than sex.* And what if someone had seen them? Not possible. Not likely.

Breathe. In. Breathe. Out.

She would deal with this. She googled her local panel beater and booked her car in for the next day, but to drive home with *that* on her door and her bonnet for all to see? She felt branded all over again. Like she needed to wash and wash, but no matter how hard she tried, she couldn't get the stain off her skin.

She eyed the small tattoo. She'd kept her promise to herself. She hadn't been pissed and she hadn't been stupid. She'd been powerful and strong. *It's okay. It's fine. Let's get to work.*

Scarlet lowered her coffee cup to her desk and eyed the teetering stack of files. Why did it all suddenly seem insurmountable? Like no matter how hard she worked, there would always be more. Endlessly more. She booted the computer, typed her password and waited for the home screen to appear. With a sip of her coffee, she opened her electronic diary and ran her eyes over her crammed-full schedule for the day ahead.

"Hi there. Are you okay?"

Scarlet looked up and Tony was there, his eyes as blue as the summer sky. His charcoal suit fitted him to perfection and her body heated. He wore a crisp white shirt and her hands itched and thrummed with memories of the hard curve of his pecs, his broad shoulders, his chest, his ripped abs. His man-nipples tightened and strained against the smooth fabric of his shirt and her body heated and liquefied. She eyed his tie—scarlet with fine violet stripes—and yearned to pull him close with it, to press her lips against the heat of his. Her mouth dried. Her tongue felt thick and awkward. She fought to swallow against the sand in her throat. "Yes, fine. Thanks…" She lifted her gaze to his eyes and gulped. "…for asking."

"Did the security cameras catch anything? Have you heard from Bob?"

His eyes spoke of something he couldn't say in an office of law and her body reacted. She squirmed in her seat. "No. Not yet."

"Can I see you later? We need to talk."

"Of course. Okay." A thousand needle pricks punctured her skin.

"Great." He gave her a wink and closed the door.

Scarlet sat and stared at her schedule for a long moment.

Her body thrummed with unwanted sensations and emotions and the words swam in front of her eyes until they crystallised and came into focus. She had a mention in how long? Fifteen minutes! She swiped a file from the top of the closest stack and opened it up. Her reading comprehension was exceptional—usually—but she found herself visualising a beach and moonlight and a naked man with a polished, statuesque body, only he wasn't cold or made of stone and she was wrapped around him like seaweed.

*Snap out of it, Scarlet. Get it together. Work. Focus.*

She forced herself to read the words, to make her notes and then she realised she was late. She was never late. She rushed to the stairwell, then realised she didn't have time to walk ten flights. She retraced her steps and stood in front of the lift. The doors opened and she schooled her breath. *You can do this.* She stepped forward and just as the doors were about to close, a man-hand and an arm pushed in. She yelped, her heart staccato-thrashing against her ribs.

"Almost missed it." Tony. Tony's voice.

The bang in her chest eased, flared again. A different kind of percussion. The doors closed and she stood there with her back against the wall. Alone. With a man. In a lift. Panic rose from somewhere deep in her belly and her vision blurred. "Please, don't press the stop button." Her words were a whisper. A frantic whisper. But his gaze said he knew how she felt. He knew what pounded inside her, and he took her in his arms.

"It's okay, Scarlet. You're safe with me. I would never hurt you. Ever. I wanted to tell you how much being with you last night meant to me. And that word scratched into your car? I would never think that of you. Ever. It wasn't like that."

"What... was it like?"

"Amazing. Special."

"For me, too." She must have smiled because he smiled back. He cupped her face in his hands and settled his lips on hers. She closed her eyes and that small, enclosed cavity opened and spread. The night sky shone above them. Vast and endless and spacious. And a part of her—that tightly wound, eyes-scrunched part of her—relaxed just a smidge. His tongue tasted and soothed and it relaxed her a bit more. He dragged her closer, file and all, and she eased into him, her body like heated syrup.

"You have courage, honey. More than anyone knows."

"I do," she said, her mouth a hair's breadth from his. "Thank you."

"You're welcome." He stepped back and winked as the lift doors opened and the cool air of the foyer rushed in. "See you when you get back."

She smiled. The doors closed and took him back to level ten and she walked with light steps towards the County Court on William Street. She enjoyed the breath of the wind and the touch of the sun where it penetrated the densely packed buildings and shone on the footpath. She was still light-hearted when she returned an hour later. She went to enter the stairwell and changed her mind. She'd take the lift. Her butt wouldn't thank her, but her tightly packed schedule would.

It was when she checked her emails several minutes later that an odd subject line caught her eye. The matter of S. L. v U. T. What was it? Her stomach clenched and she broke out in a cold sweat. Her hand shook as she manoeuvred the mouse and clicked on the item in her inbox.

Photos stared back at her. Photos of two people, wet and naked in the ocean. Two people in a very compromising position. A close-up of their bodies joined, ecstasy and pain on her face. Ecstasy and pain on Tony's. Below the photos was a demand. *Back off, slut. I want your resignation on Daniel Wigmore's desk by ten o'clock tomorrow morning, or this email will be forwarded to each and every one of the equity partners and your career is history. Done. No firm will want you. You're a liability. A slut. No man is safe around you.*

Scarlet's stomach heaved and she dry-retched. She backed away from her desk like a python had uncurled and slipped from the monitor. Who could have done this? How could anyone but Tony have known? Had he orchestrated the whole thing to get rid of her? Did he want the position that badly? But how could he have known they'd end up together, unless… was she that pathetic? Did she look that desperate? He'd promised nothing would happen. It had been her decision to take it further. Hadn't it? Or had he used reverse psychology to get what he wanted? The events of the night before played out in her mind, over and over. None of it made sense. The photos were real enough.

She stepped closer to the monitor and sought the sender's address. It was a generic one. Nothing specific. Nothing to give away the identity of the sender. Probably sent from a local library or internet café. Whoever had sent them was smart enough to cover their tracks. The bastard was no doubt responsible for the damage to her car as well.

She fumed and stormed and cussed from one end of her office to the other. What now? What should she do? There was no way she would allow herself to be blackmailed. No way she would give whoever it was that kind of power over her. She didn't know if Tony was involved, but he was certainly the main beneficiary if she resigned and *that* spoke volumes.

If it wasn't Tony, it had to be Geoffrey. The guy hated her.

Blamed her for his own weakness and the destruction of his marriage. Never mind that he'd been a partner and she'd been a lowly receptionist, so fresh and new to the business she'd had no clue that lowlifes like him existed. Well, she'd learned, and she'd fought, and she'd won. There was no way she'd allow him to push her down now.

She pictured him the day before, his face twisted with hate. This wasn't a coincidence. He blamed Scarlet for his own bad behaviour. The only question was whether Geoffrey had gone rogue, or if Tony had been in on the plot?

Geoffrey must have followed them, but why? Because he didn't want Tony succeeding where he'd failed? Well, boo hoo Mr. Big Shot. Tony was a hundred times the man Geoffrey was. A thousand times. Unless he'd known. Unless they'd concocted the plot together. Kill two birds with one stone? Revenge and clear the path to the partnership position Tony wanted so badly. But his father had died. There was no need to impress him anymore. Or perhaps that hadn't been true either. Perhaps that had been a sob-story to weaken her.

She didn't know. The light at the periphery of her vision became watery and flashy and pain stabbed in her temple. Her stomach shifted and adrenaline raced. She hadn't had a migraine since her early twenties, but she'd suffered badly from them when she was younger. She reached into her drawer for paracetamol, picked up her phone and called her legal assistant. "Trace, I've got the mother of all migraines brewing. Could you please come in and go through my diary? Postpone what you can."

She eyed the photos on her screen and took out a USB drive. She saved a copy of the email and the photos before deleting them from her computer. She didn't want anyone to find them.

Dark spots floated like ghouls in her vision. It wasn't safe to drive. She ordered an Uber, then threw her bag over her shoulder and headed for the lift, her vision swimming.

"Scarlet."

Tony's voice. From the distance. Near blinded, she pushed on. Thunderous waves thudded in her head. "Migraine," she muttered. "Going home."

"I'll take you."

"No need. I've ordered an Uber." Every cell in her body seized. Friend or foe?

"I'll come around later and check that you're okay."

"I'm okay."

"You don't look okay. You look grey. Pale." He accompanied her into the lift. "What happened? You were fine."

"I was." She closed her eyes and leaned against the mirrored wall. Her head felt like it had split down the middle. The right side of her face felt numb. Her arm, too. If he knew about the photos, he was a good actor. He played the chivalrous love-interest to perfection. He helped her out to the car and held the door while she settled into the back.

"Call me when you get home." He slammed the door and she eased her head back, her eyes closed against the blinding light.

# Chapter Seven

When Scarlet opened her eyes the next morning, she saw it was after seven. She was late. Two mornings in a row? She sat upright and the room spun. She waited for the awful sensation to steady and subside. She'd thrown up before she'd retreated into sleep—a deep, dark sleep—and she needed a shower. She padded to the bathroom and stood under the hot spray for a good while, shampooing her hair and washing away the faint scent of sickness. She smoothed conditioner over it and used an exfoliating mitt to soap herself while she waited the obligatory sixty seconds before washing the conditioner out.

Every wipe of the mitt brought a wave of memories. Of lathering up with Tony. Of touching and smoothing her hands over his incredible body. And it was then, when her mind turned to the ocean, that she remembered. Her hand stilled. Her blood ran cold. Her mind rushed to the time. Under three hours. She had under three hours to work out what to do. The equity partners couldn't see the photos. Not if she wanted to keep her job and her credibility.

She should tell Tony. Confront him.

But he might pretend he knew nothing about it or worse, come to her rescue and she'd believe he was on her side... when maybe he wasn't. She cringed as she fought the shame. She wasn't a gullible nineteen-year-old anymore. Where could a relationship with Tony go anyway? He wanted the position she wanted. And imagine Christmas lunch. Family events. She'd have to face Geoffrey over the dinner table and pretend she was fine with it when she wasn't fine with it. She wasn't fine with the hatred in his eyes or the suggestion that she'd seduced him, when in truth, he'd preyed upon her. She wasn't fine with the shame. She could hardly have ignored Geoffrey and told him to piss off. It was her first job. She was good at it. Why should she have given it up because her boss was a jerk? As it turned out, she'd given it up anyway.

"Are you planning to stay in there all day?"

Her heart near bounced off the ceiling. "Jesus, Radcliff. Is that you?"

"You let me in. Last night. I didn't want you to be alone. How are you feeling? Last time I saw you, you looked like death. You slept like the dead, too."

"Oh, I didn't remember. Thank you, I'm a lot better this morning." Her cheeks burned.

"I've made you some eggs on toast and a green smoothie."

His voice washed over her like warm caramel and her tears mingled with the droplets of water from the shower. "And coffee?"

"Yes, coffee was top of the list." She heard a smile in his tone.

"Would you mind passing me a towel?"

"I've seen you naked before, honey."

"Not today you haven't, Radcliff." He placed the towel in her outstretched hand, and she pulled it behind the rippled glass screen. He'd brought fire and brimstone into her life. Or maybe he'd just stirred the embers.

"See you when you're ready."

"Give me five minutes."

"There you are." Tony glanced up from his cooking and assessed her. "You look pale. Are you okay?"

He slid a poached egg onto toast slathered with avocado and looked very much at home in her French provincial-style kitchen. "I will be."

He pushed a freshly brewed coffee towards her, and it was hard to hate him. She closed her hands around the porcelain cup, taking a deep breath of the rich, full scent. He was a victim here, too. He just didn't know it...or maybe he did. Maybe he didn't care. Maybe she had more to lose than he did. She settled herself onto one of the stools at the marble island bench and took a sip.

"Are you well enough to go into work?" Tony took a swig of his coffee. "I'm meeting with Geoffrey to get dad's funeral sorted today so I won't be in."

"What time's your meeting?" The word brought a wave of nausea to her stomach and the fight drained out of her. The equity partners couldn't see the photos. She didn't want her reputation ruined... again. She didn't want to feel ashamed... again. She couldn't face it. She didn't want to. She didn't have to. She could resign.

"Eleven."

"I *will* go in." She toyed with her food and watched him devour his share. She could get a job elsewhere. If Geoffrey didn't sabotage that, too. It would set her timeframe back. Who knew when she'd make partner? Unlike Tony, her name wouldn't be enough to entice head-hunters or mess with the pecking order. She'd have to earn her stripes all over again. Long hours. No weekends off. She'd seen a light at the end of the tunnel and now it was gone.

"Here. Try the smoothie. Your body needs hydration. Protein, too."

She felt exhausted. "Why do you care? Why are you here?"

"I thought that was obvious."

The revolt of her thoughts collided with the warmth in his eyes. "There's no need. It was one night. I'm a big girl, Radcliff. You're off the hook."

"There is no hook. I'm here because I want to be. We made love, O'Connor. We're not done yet." He lowered his cup to the bench.

Sexy man-shadow peppered his jaw and there was the trap of those dimples. She gave them a wide berth. "We're more than done."

He stepped around the bench and turned her stool until she fitted between his thighs. He took her face in his hands and her heart along with it, his blue, blue gaze blazing. He closed the distance between them, and his mouth settled on hers, hot and hungry. She fought the magic even as she sank into his kiss. Even as she felt those waves buffeting her body. Even as his arms wrapped around her and her heart sighed along with his.

When his mouth lifted from hers, his gaze was steady. "We're not done."

"Do me a favour and tell Geoffrey that when you see him." Her insides squeezed with a different kind of emotion. She pushed Tony back and turned to eat the breakfast he'd made for her.

"I will." He moved to the other side of the bench and watched as she ate, returning his attention to his own food. "I like your house. It's an extension of you. Stylish. Everything in its place." He cut his toast and egg. "We'll have to go through Dad's things today. I'm not looking forward to it."

"It's a difficult time for you."

"It is." He paused, his fork halfway to his mouth. "What is it, O'Connor?"

"I think I may have to resign."

"Resign? Why? Not on my account. We can work together. I love your competent lawyer-mode. It's incredibly sexy."

He smiled and there were those dimples, deep enough to fall into. "You want the promotion."

"Of course, I do. And you want it, too." He took a sip of his coffee. "I didn't have you pegged as a quitter."

"I'm not sure the cost is worth it." Her mouth was tinder-dry, and her insides fluttered. She wanted to believe him. She wanted to trust him, but…

"What cost? Work is work. After work is after work." He lowered his cutlery, his forehead creasing. "I don't have a problem with that. If you get the promotion, then you earned it. If I get the promotion, then I earned it."

"It's not that simple."

"It should be."

"You're right. It should be." She lifted her coffee, took a sip and eyed him over the rim.

His gaze snapped to her wrist. "What does the PS truly stand for?"

Scarlet glanced down and the ink swam before her eyes. "Pissed and Stupid. That's why I don't get drunk. I don't go to office parties. I thought I'd learned my lesson. But this…"

"We can manage this. I don't want *this* to go away. *This* is the best thing that's happened to me… ever." His blue gaze blazed, and he took her hand in his.

"It isn't right."

"Oh, trust me. It's more than right." He squeezed her hand, then lifted it to his mouth. His kiss was slow and sexy and if she hadn't seen the photos, she would have fallen for it.

"Thanks for breakfast." She pulled her hand back and stood. "I need to get ready for work."

"I had your car towed to the local repair shop. They said you'd already booked it in for today." He threw her a set of keys. "And I organised a hire car for you. It's out the front. Would you like me to drop you off or would you rather go in alone?"

"I'd rather go in alone if that's okay." She picked up her plate and carried it to the sink. She studied the row of perfectly spaced Ficus trees outside the window and the promise of another sunny day.

"No problem. I'll take my bike."

"It's here?" Her words were out, naked and panicked before she'd had time to smooth the edges. Oh, no. Geoffrey would know he'd stayed the night. Her skin prickled and her breakfast shifted in her stomach…

"What's wrong, O'Connor? We promised each other honesty. Bald, bad-arse, tough-as-you-like honesty." His gaze seared. "What's going on?"

Inside, she oscillated. Trust him. Don't trust him. Trust him. Don't trust him.

He lowered his fork and strode over to her, taking her into his arms. She resisted. Part of her resisted. The rest of her melted like butter on hot toast. He held her. Tight. Close. Like he never wanted to let her go. And the tears started. Hot, scalding tears on her cheek, on his shirt. Yesterday's shirt? It smelt of him. Musky. Sweet. Salty. And she sobbed. Because she wanted to trust him. She wanted to think he couldn't do this, but what if he could?

He tipped her chin up to study her and his eyes were clear. There was confusion and hurt and vulnerability. She raised herself up on her toes to press her lips to his, to taste, to lose herself in his warmth. His hands ran over her back, bringing her closer, fitting her against his hard ridges and planes. Her body reacted like a flame to a fuse—hungry, hurried and hopeful. Home. He felt like home.

When he pushed her back, his gaze demanded the truth.

"I received an email with photos, compromising photos... of us... in the ocean. It demanded that I resign by ten o'clock today, or the photos would be sent to all of the equity partners."

Tony reeled away as if she'd slapped him and his eyes flashed blue flame. "What?"

Scarlet took a deep breath and steadied the shaking in her limbs. "I think Geoffrey might be responsible, but I don't know."

"When?"

"Yesterday. That's what triggered my migraine."

"When were you planning to tell me?" He glared at her. "You weren't planning to tell me. You were going to resign? You were going to walk away from everything you've worked so hard to achieve. Because of a threat? Without telling me why. We had a pact, O'Connor." Pain shone in his eyes.

He was right. She hadn't trusted him. He'd been kind and honest and caring. And now, the clear blue depths of his eyes harboured icebergs. Giant, shadowy conglomerates that threatened to fracture the fragile connection that remained between them, frayed and fraught. "I'm sorry. My head was in a spin. Literally. I panicked. I couldn't think. I still can't."

"I'm sorry, too. Show me."

"Okay." She walked over to the soft pink wingback chair in her study where she'd dumped her handbag and fished out the

81

USB. With shaking hands, she waited for her laptop to boot up. Her gaze leapt from the white marble fireplace mantle to the silk lilies in their vase, to the dark timber floor and back to her wild reflection in the giant gilt mirror above the mantle. Tony stood behind her, dark and livid like a thundercloud, his jaw tight, his eyes glued to the screen. She logged in, slipped the USB into place and opened the document.

Rigid was too tame a term for the man who stood petrified into cold stone beside her.

Bile rose in her throat as she scrolled through the photos.

The only sounds were the harsh intake and exhale of Tony's breath, and the dull thud of her own pulse.

"You thought I had something to do with this?"

Scarlet grappled with her thoughts. Honesty. They'd promised honesty. "The thought crossed my mind. I didn't want to believe it, but with me out of the running, you'd get a free pass at partnership."

He held her shoulders and turned her towards him, his gaze scathing. "I had nothing to do with this. *Nothing.* It's stalking. It's perverted. It's wrong at so many levels."

"I don't see how I can fight this. I don't want to show the email to Dan. I couldn't bear the innuendo. I would lose all credibility. Whatever way this unfolds… I lose. Geoffrey wins. It's about revenge."

"And I'm Geoffrey's brother." He looked at her with despair in his eyes. "I understand now. Yet you kissed me. You trusted me enough to show me these."

"Yes."

"I think I might love you, O'Connor." His gaze smouldered and her heart expanded until her chest ached.

"I think I could love you, too, Radcliff, but I don't see how…"

"Phone into work and tell them you're sick."

Her eyes widened. "Why."

"We're going to see Geoffrey. Together. Before ten o'clock."

"What if it's a random stalker? An unhappy client? A disgruntled employee at work?"

"Then it's a train wreck we can't stop. I'll stand by you. We face this together. Both of us are in those photos. Both of us have been violated." He took her into his arms and held her close. His warmth soaked into her and soothed her frazzled nerves, setting her heart aflame.

"I like you. More than I should." She pressed her cheek against the soft sateen cotton of his shirt, felt the hard curve of his chest, the rhythmic thud of his heart right there. Solid and safe.

"I like you, too. And we'll deal with this together." He sealed the vow with a kiss that stole her breath.

Given the right set of circumstances, a man was capable of murder. Tony's hands itched with the need to clench tightly around his brother's throat and crush his windpipe.

Given the right set of circumstances, blood between brothers could turn bad. The thought of his brother touching Scarlet against her will razed him to ashes. Injustice added to insult added to injury. It wasn't possible to hate his brother any more than he did right now. He reeled with the bitterness of it.

Given the right set of circumstances, *a man could want revenge.* Geoffrey was a sad, weak, pathetic human being. But their father was dead. And Geoffrey had taken it hard.

The fury that had whipped his body into a hornet's nest blew itself out. It was like stumbling in the dark. Their father had been a strong beacon for what was right, what to look out for, when to beware. He'd dictated his brother's path, even more so than his own. If *he* felt lost? How did Geoffrey feel? Hurt.

Deeply hurt. And his MO was to blame someone else. To take it out on them. Tony's grip on Scarlet's hand tightened.

Geoffrey lived in East Melbourne in an expensive townhouse and it was a blessing they'd been caught in traffic along Flinders Street. It had given him time for his anger to ratchet up to an indignant height before blowing itself out. His brother was alone. His wife had left him years ago. His kids hated him. He'd reaped what he'd sown. Lonely wealth.

Tony's eyes stung with tears. *Men don't cry, Anthony. Men toughen up and get on with the job.*

# Chapter Eight

Tony stood at Geoffrey's door with his hand raised. Scarlet stood beside him. But the door flew open before he could knock.

"How could you bring your slut here?" His brother puffed up like a toxic toad, his fists clenched, his forehead pulled into an angry point between his brows.

"*She* is the woman I'm going to marry one day and if you ever... ever... call her a slut again, or touch her car, or threaten her in any way, I will kill you with my bare hands."

Geoffrey reeled as if he'd been slapped and stepped back.

"You're a despicable human being and if you send those photos to Dan, I will never speak to you again. You will never meet our children and the legal community will know what you did. I'll make sure of it. You will lose the respect of your peers and we'll sue you for defamation. Stalking. Blackmail." He pulled out his phone. "I'll report you to the police. You'll lose your practicing certificate. Your choice. Now."

"You always were pathetic." Geoffrey's lip curled. "You're the one who wanted to be partner by thirty and prove that you were better than me. I was just making it easier for you. Two birds. One stone. You should be thanking me."

"No, *Dad* wanted me to be partner by thirty. *I* wanted Dad's respect. I wanted *your* respect. Not your devious help to cheat someone I admire. A lot." A laugh started deep in his gut. "I couldn't care *less* about the partnership position and I couldn't care *less* about what you think of me because I don't think much of you. You're lonely and miserable because of *your* choices. *Your* actions. And until you appreciate that, no one can help you. The only person to blame is yourself. *Not* Scarlet. You've been the best possible role model in the worst possible way."

His brother's scowl deepened. The sun shone from his bare scalp and his cheeks, ruddy with broken capillaries, flushed a deeper shade of red. His eyes, bloodshot and red-rimmed, squinted against the light. His breath reeked of alcohol and he was in the same clothes he'd worn when he took Tony to the hospital to say goodbye to their father.

"Don't you see. Dad's death was a blessing. A reprieve from a disease that would have stolen his dignity—slowly—before it mercilessly took his life. He's with mum. He's better off there. That doesn't make it hurt any less. Nor does it mean I don't miss him. I do." Emotion snaked into his throat and Tony swallowed against it. "But it's selfish not to be relieved for him."

"You went straight to her."

"Scarlet made it bearable. Better than seeking solace in a bottle."

"Geoffrey…" Scarlet's voice was quiet and kind and strong, and it was like a release valve to his temper. There was more at stake here than his own hurt feelings.

"You're hurting. I can see that and I'm sorry for your loss."

Tony squeezed her hand and she lifted her chin.

"But I don't deserve your animosity. I didn't deserve it when I was nineteen and I don't deserve it now. I'm a good lawyer. A good person. I want you to pay for my car repairs and I want your word that those photos will never see the light of day. I want an apology."

His brother reached out for the door but instead of slamming it shut in their faces, he slumped against it and cried, his big, overweight body racked by sobs, loud and wrenching.

Scarlet stepped forward and rested her hand on his shoulder. Tony's eyes stung and his throat closed with the pain of seeing the woman he wanted most in his life console the man who'd taken so much from hers.

He moved forward and wrapped his arms around Scarlet, his nose breathing in the sweetness of her silky, smooth hair, his lips lowering to kiss the glossy golden strands before he moved to comfort his brother, their embrace one of mutual loss. Raw and intense. For the first time, he allowed himself the freedom to feel it. To cry. To sob. Not to lessen it. Not to ignore it. Not to dull it with something or someone else.

*I'll miss you, dad. I loved you. Not enough. Not nearly enough. But I loved you. I admired you. I respected you. In the beginning. In the end. If not in the middle.*

"I'll make tea." Scarlet's voice came to him from a distance.

He caught her gaze over his brother's head and nodded. "Thank you." Geoffrey shook in his arms, his cries high pitched like a child's. Tony rubbed Geoffrey's back and he held on like a man drowning. "It'll be okay. We'll be okay."

Scarlet lowered a pot of tea and cups onto the glass coffee table and poured them each a cup. He pulled away from his brother and his heart swelled with her calm efficiency. She settled on the edge of the leather sofa, her legs crossed, her expression controlled.

Geoffrey's gaze was watery. "I'm sorry, Scarlet. I am. For all of it. For following you both. For taking the photos. For using them against you. For the car." He looked down, his face reddening. "But it's too late."

"What do you mean, it's too late?" Tony growled.

"I've already sent the photos."

Scarlet nodded and held her tea with a shaking hand, her face pale, her eyes wet.

"You said ten o'clock." Tony's eyes narrowed. "You sent them anyway. When? When did you send them?"

"Last night."

"You wanted to ruin her reputation. To take her down because in your own small mind, that's what she did to you. This was about revenge?"

"I wanted her to blame you. You were the one with the most to gain. I wanted her to reject you the way she rejected me. I'm not proud of it."

Tony bit his lip, his mind whirling. How the hell could he fix this? He watched as Scarlet took a sip of her tea, her movements slow. Her gaze clung to the carpeted floor. He was responsible for bringing Geoffrey back into her life and his brother had hurt her again. He feared their relationship was dead in the water. "This was my fault, Scarlet. This was about me. Not about you."

She lowered her cup to the glass table in front of her seat and her violet eyes stormed. "I'm a woman. I'm held to a different standard of behaviour. This won't hurt you the way it will hurt me." She stood and wiped the moisture from her eyes. "I need to go to the office and deal with this."

"I'll drive you." Tony jumped to his feet. He dug into his pocket for the hire car key. "We'll face Dan together. I don't expect you to care a whit about me after this, but if you'll have me, I want you to know I'm in it for the long haul."

"Wait." Geoffrey rose from the couch. "Give me five minutes, Scarlet. I need a shower. I'll tell Dan what happened and who was responsible. I'll fix this."

"You could lose your practicing certificate if he takes it to the authorities," Tony said.

"I could." Geoffrey swiped his nose with the back of his hand. "But I was wrong and I'm ashamed of myself. Dad would be ashamed of me, too. I apologise, Scarlet, I do. And I apologise for my behaviour all those years ago. I took advantage of your kindness and your naivety and worse, I blamed you when it all went wrong."

Scarlet nodded, her back strong. She looked beautiful and dignified and... powerful. Tony salivated. His body heated. His hunger rose. And he saw it there, reflected in her eyes. She felt it, too. This connection. This need. He didn't see Geoffrey step away, his back curved. He didn't see the excessive wealth around him. And he didn't see partnership in his near future, but he saw it in Scarlet's eyes where their future shone like the sun on a rare, precious flower.

"You're seduction in a suit, O'Connor."

"You're pretty sexy yourself, Radcliff." She smiled and her face glowed.

"Let's wait in the garden. The open space is calling to me."

"I'm kind of partial to it myself," she said, and her palm slid against his. Who would have thought that holding hands could be so evocative?

"Thank you," he murmured, his lips close to hers. The scent of gardenias was strong in the warm air. "I'm sorry my dad didn't get to meet you. He would have liked you."

"Are you okay? I don't know how I'd breathe if my dad passed away."

"I would be there for you. Holding you. Making it bearable. The same way you're making it bearable for me." He closed the gap and savoured the feel of her lips against his. Petal soft. And sweet. Deliciously sweet. He settled into the kiss, the heat of it. Deep and long and hypnotic. He didn't know how he'd breathe without her.

"Thank you."

He lifted his head and his gaze fell into the violet magic of hers. "For what?"

"You've helped me to put the past to rest. Helped me to breathe in a lift and to see what's important. It's not how much you earn or how powerful you are, but rather how you feel about yourself and how you appear through the eyes of those you love."

"Are you saying you love me, O'Connor?"

"That would be premature after two days, Radcliff."

"Two days, two minutes, two decades... makes no difference to me. My heart knows already that you're the only woman I'll ever want. A partnership with you is the only partnership that matters to me."

"A partnership for life?" She smiled and her gaze filled with unshed tears. "I'd like that with you."

"But?"

"But those carefree kids of yours who run loose on the beach?" Her smile collapsed at the edges and her eyes turned cool and bleak.

"The ones with the blonde hair and the violet-blue eyes and the smiles exactly like yours?" He wiped her cheek, his gaze captured by the smooth texture of her skin, the sparkle of the sun on her tears like two stars reflected from the heavens.

"I have endometriosis. My mum had it, too. She couldn't get

pregnant again after she had me. She said she left it too late." Scarlet's gaze dropped from his. "What if I can't have children? What if I can't give you those carefree kids? I want them for you. I want them for us. You would make an amazing dad."

"Ah. The real reason behind the rush to partnership."

"The older I get, the greater the risk I won't be able to get pregnant."

"Then, we'd better get practising, honey, because without you, those kids mean nothing. What are we waiting for?"

"Me." Geoffrey's voice sounded from the doorway. "Are you two lovebirds ready?"

"Yes, I think we are." Tony's voice was triumphant. "We have an important merger to discuss. I'll drop you at the office. You can handle the rest on your own, right?"

"Yes. I got you both into this mess and I'll get you both out of it."

"Excellent." Tony captured Scarlet's hand and wrapped an arm around Geoffrey. "How long since you've seen your kids? It's amazing how powerful an apology can be."

"Don't we have a funeral to arrange?"

"Nope. More of a celebration of dad's life. What about Torquay? Let's spread his ashes under the night sky. It's the closest place to heaven I know." After being in Scarlet's arms... but he hardly needed to share that with Geoffrey. Instead, he squeezed Scarlet's hand and caught her watery gaze, held it, and shared what was in his heart.

"Is that why you headed there the other night?" His brother's voice pulled him back from a place beyond heaven.

"Yep. You should try looking upwards and outwards some time, Bro. You're missing out on something special." He pulled Scarlet closer beside him. Held onto her like a man drowning.

"I'm missing out on some*one* special, that's for sure." His brother crumpled, his overweight body pulling forwards, his shoulders rounded. Gone was the smell of alcohol that had reeked from his pores, but his ruddy flesh and puffy eyes told a different story.

"There are a million fish in the sea."

"Hey, I'm still here," said Scarlet with a laugh. "And I like to think I'm one of a kind."

"You're the only one for me," Tony said with a grin and a wink, but he was the most serious he'd ever been in his life.

Tony pulled into a parking space in front of the office in Collins St. The traffic pulsed and throbbed, frenetic around them. He'd forgotten it was a workday. He waited until Geoffrey slammed the rear door and started to walk towards the building, his shoulders slumped, his steps slow. But then he straightened and turned and waved, and Tony waved back. He glanced in the mirror and waited for a break in the snarl of traffic. "And now, Miss O'Connor. We have an important matter to attend to."

"We do?"

"One that doesn't involve a legal file or a business suit, although you wear those better than most." He reached out and took her hand in his.

"I think I like where you're going with this."

She smiled and he could have swum in the violet sea of her eyes for the rest of his days. "I definitely like where I'm going with this, and I know you will too. I'll make sure of it."

# Epilogue

"Sunscreen!" Scarlet called after her two rascally four-year-old sons who zipped away, their grins wide, their surfboards under their arms. She lowered the tube and locked eyes with Tony.

"Don't sweat it, honey. It's after five o'clock. They won't burn. Besides, they have my skin. They're fine." His lopsided smile was hard to resist, particularly when his chest was bare and he was half clad in a wetsuit, his board under his arm.

"Come on, Dad." Two voices, identical in tone. Impatient.

"Why don't you have a rest until Geoff, Ally, and the kids arrive?"

Scarlet rested her hand on her swollen belly. "Your daughter would love that. It's when I lie down that she practices her surfing moves."

"Well, she has two older brothers to keep up with."

He grinned and her body reacted, a wave of heat washing through her.

"Or if you'd rather, we could curl up together." His blue, blue eyes gleamed and he stepped closer, his hand framing her jaw, his lips like heated velvet against hers.

"Someone needs to keep those two, safe." She looked beyond him to where the waves broke against the sand and their sons had already launched onto their boards, waving and shouting for Tony to hurry up. She smiled and her heart filled with love—overwhelming, gut-wrenching love, but it was when her gaze returned to his adoring one that the tears began to swell. "Hormones," she grumbled and wiped the wetness with an impatient hand.

"I love you, O'Connor. Every minute of every day."

"I love you, too." She sank into his kiss, a space opening inside her as wide and as deep as the ocean, as vast and as endless as the night sky. A space filled with love and desire, and hope.

"Dad!"

"Gotta go." He dragged his lips from hers, his gaze devouring her. "You look good."

"I look huge."

"You look perfect." He planted another kiss on her lips and turned to chase after the boys.

Scarlet sat at her desk, her mind on her closing argument for an arbitration on Monday, when the door opened, and Geoffrey called out.

"I thought partners got the weekend off. Especially pregnant ones."

She turned and welcomed him with a smile. "As you well know, there's no such thing as time off in this business."

"Well, there should be. Besides, haven't you got your hands full with your two little monkeys. Where are they?"

"In the surf with their dad. They won't be long. Ah, here they are now." The screen door banged, and two wet, blond-haired boys stormed into the room bringing a trail of sand in with them.

"Hi, Uncle Geoff and Auntie Ally. Ethan! Georgia! You won't believe what we saw! A stingray. A big one. Swimming in the surf."

"Better a ray than a shark," Georgia said with a laugh, ruffling Thomas's hair. She was in her twenties but adored her younger cousins.

"It was huge, but it didn't try to attack us."

"It was surfing, too," Jacob added.

"Where's your dad?" Scarlet asked.

"Right here." Tony grinned and shook hands with his brother. "Good to see you guys. Hey, kids. How are things?"

"Really good! Can we take the boys out for a game of beach cricket?"

"Go for it. We'll get the dinner happening and then your dad and I will challenge you to a match. You need all the practice you can get if memory serves me right. Too easy," he said to Geoffrey with a grin.

"Not a chance," they called, their voices jeering in unison. "No way. We'll beat you this time!"

"How are you feeling?" Alison asked Scarlet.

"Fine. Tired. I'm looking forward to Eve's arrival. How about you?"

"Busy. If it wasn't for Geoff, I'd be at the office, but I'm glad I'm here. Every time we come down; I love it more. And it's great to see you all."

Scarlet and Alison carried the bread and the salad outside and placed them on the table before relaxing into a couple of chairs. Scarlet poured them both an iced water and they sat back to chat.

"We've firmed up on our decision to retire from the practice. We'll do some consultant work, but we want to spend more time at our house down here and travel. I feel like I've spent the best part of my life at work."

Scarlet glanced over at Geoffrey who looked back at them and winked at Alison. He was far from the man she'd known. He held a glass of iced water and he'd trimmed down. He no longer drank alcohol and looked better for it. The smell of perfectly cooked meat filled the air. Geoffrey and Tony's talk was punctuated with laughter.

The kids abandoned their game and moved on to a version of chasey. They ran across the sand, the big kids whooping as joyfully as the little ones.

"Meat's ready," Tony called over to her.

"I'll get the kids," Geoffrey said.

Alison rose with a warm smile. "I'll come with you. I'd like to stretch my legs." They held hands as they stepped off the patio and onto the sand.

Scarlet stood, too, and Tony came up behind her, wrapping his arms around her.

"This is just what I pictured. This is just how I hoped it would be. Kids. Family. Fun on the beach. The smell of the barbecue. You—my love, my always."

He kissed her neck and breathed against the sensitive skin there sending delicious ripples of desire through every cell. She leaned against him, her gaze on the gulls that winged through the air with elated cries. The sun was low in the sky, and the horizon was washed with rose-pink, mauve, and orange. The boys ran towards their Uncle, their voices joyful and Alison wrapped her arm around Georgia's shoulder.

Scarlet rested her hand on her firm, round belly and Tony rested his hand on hers. Their daughter stretched and turned.

"This is more, so much more, than I dared to hope for," Scarlet whispered, and Tony pulled her close.

\* \* \*

Thank you so much for reading Bachelor on Trial! I hope you enjoyed the story. I really enjoyed writing it. I met Mr. G at a wedding, and I fell in love with him at first sight. He was down to earth and honest and there was a deep connection. I loved the juxtaposition of clean-shaven, serious lawyer, and adventure-loving bikie in a leather jacket and jeans. I'd never been on a motorbike and I was afraid and in love in equal parts. He loved camping trips with his bikie mates and the outdoors, and I loved the whole package!

Your honest review would be very much appreciated on Amazon (your website of choice) and/or on Goodreads: https://www.goodreads.com/book/show/55549115-bachelor-on-trial. Authors rely on readers' reviews to stand out from the pack (hopefully in a good way)!

I'd love to hear how you and your partner met and what attracted you!

You can find me at www.lexigreene.com.au or on facebook at www.facebook.com/lexi.greene.75 or www.facebook.com/lovelexigreene or via email at lexigreene@aapt.net.au.

Warmest regards,

Lexi xx

# About the Author

Lexi is an Australian author who loves to write powerful, passionate, and provocative stories. She writes romance in the early morning and works as a paediatric neuropsychologist by day. A happily married mum of two teens, a parrot, and a puppy, she loves to escape into a good story. She is a firm believer that a bath, a green tea, and chocolate take a good book and make it perfect.

Lexi is a member of Romance Writers of Australia and Romance Writers of America, and she is a huge fan of Margie Lawson's Writer's Academy.

Lexi loves a good happily ever after...

**You can connect with me on:**
- 🌐 https://lexigreene.com.au
- 🐦 https://twitter.com/lexi_greene
- 📘 https://facebook.com/lexi.greene.75

**Subscribe to my newsletter:**

✉ https://dl.bookfunnel.com/lzmhskru7g

# Also by Lexi Greene

**Bachelor on Board**
Success is the best revenge.

Amber Reed, a rising television producer, needs her new show—Bachelor on Board, Australia—to outshine the one her ex stole from her, or risk losing her job to the conniving Lothario, but when her Bachelor falls in love and absconds with one of the contestants, she's forced to rely on Plan B, Nathan Moretti, the high school popular who broke her heart.

Nathan Moretti, soon-to-be head of the wealthy Moretti family, needs a wife to protect the family fortune from his gold-digger stepmother, and his job should be easy with twenty-four beautiful women to choose from. Right?

Not when the only woman he wants is the one behind the camera and her success relies on him finding love with someone else, on screen, on schedule, as promised. Can Amber forgive the past and risk her heart—again?

**https://books2read.com/Bachelor-On-Board**

**Bachelor on Guard**

Abby Kercher has spent the past five years proving she doesn't need Nico D'Antoni, but now her life is in danger and Nico is the only man who can keep her safe.

Abby is all grown up and Nico finds she's changed in dangerous ways, but some things haven't changed, like their unwanted attraction, the darkness of his past, and his promise to protect her, which must override everything.

Can they put their past behind them, or will a long-kept secret destroy them both?

**https://books2read.com/Bachelor-On-Guard**

## Once Upon a Christmas Wish

Jenn Adams is determined to tick off her bucket list and face her past nemeses—learning to ski and a man named Brad.

Brad Oregon is the only man she's ever loved. His chocolate eyes. His to-die-for smile. His toned body. His very toned body.

But Brad's reputation with women is almost as renowned as his ski-racing success. Now a ski instructor in beautiful Whistler, he's as difficult to resist as the scenery! What the hell. Life is short. A two-week holiday romance should suit them both perfectly. Right?

**https://books2read.com/Once-Upon-A-Christmas-Wish**

## Desert Prince, Scandalous Affair

There is nothing Zahidah's Prince Rashid bin Ra'ed Al Shahid won't do to safeguard his family's honour and his kingdom's future.

And there is nothing Jemma Mason won't do to protect her daughter, Sami, the result of a crazy one-night connection with a dark, handsome cliché in a Sydney bar.

When Sami needs a bone marrow transplant to save her life, Jemma must travel to Zahidah and face the prince who has no idea he's a father. But when Princess Aminah, Rashid's sister, steps in and saves Sami's life (and Jemma's secret), there is nothing Jemma won't do for Aminah including rescuing her from an arranged marriage she dreads.

When Aminah is abducted, Prince Rashid wants answers and his questions lead him to Jemma and her web of lies.

Jemma can't resist Rashid's scandalous proposal but can he forgive her when he discovers the truth?

**https://books2read.com/Desert-Prince-Scandalous-Affair**

### Shatterproof

LEXI GREENE

Emily Stone, an internationally successful model on the brink of supermodel stardom, appears to have it all. All, except love, because Emily wants the kind of man who isn't fooled by the pretty. She wants the kind of love that's big enough and true enough to include her disabled sister and dysfunctional mother.

Nick was an A-list actor in tinsel town with a super-sized ego until a tragic car accident stole his wife, his unborn child, and his gilded career, leaving him physically and emotionally scarred.

When wintry French Island brings these two wayward souls home, shared childhood memories aren't enough to bridge the deep divide forged by their adult lives and choices. That is until Carmie, Emily's delightful Down Syndrome sister, weaves her special kind of magic.

Can Carmie's boundless love and infectious joy help them to heal their broken hearts or will the glamour of Emily's work-world whisk her away?

**https://books2read.com/Heart-of-Glass-Shatterpoof**

www.ingramcontent.com/pod-product-compliance
Lightning Source LLC
Chambersburg PA
CBHW020322130626
46549CB00003B/963